Endorsements

Be prepared to catch air with a teenager from Taos, New Mexico as the hero and an Irish lass as a heroine. The Irish Skateboard Club's perilous investigations into Dublin's human trafficking kept me turning the page through that last tension-tight scene and nails a TEN with courage, humor, and - yes - romance!

—**Parris Afton Bonds,** New York Times best-selling author of *The Brigands*

The Irish Skateboard Club is a masterpiece, fast-paced and exciting! The language is spot-on and the story line is a mixture of adventure and coming-of-age, with a chilling glimpse into the internal workings of a global human trafficking ring. No age borders on this thriller! Kudos to Colenda!

—**Jacqueline Boyd,** PhD, author, former Director, Moreno Valley High School (nationally ranked charter school), Angel Fire, NM.

THE IRISH
SKATEBOARD CLUB

Other Books by the Author

The Callahan Family Saga:

Cochabamba Conspiracy

Homeland Burning

Chita Quest

Available from Southern Yellow Pine Publishing
www.syppublishing.com

THE IRISH
SKATEBOARD CLUB

BRINN COLENDA

This is a work of fiction. All of the characters, organizations, and events portrayed in this novel are either products of the author's imagination or are used fictitiously.

The Irish Skateboard Club © 2020 by Brinn Colenda.
All Rights Reserved.

Printed in the United States of America

Published by Author Academy Elite
PO Box 43, Powell, OH 43035
www.AuthorAcademyElite.com

All rights reserved. This book contains material protected under International and Federal Copyright Laws and Treaties. Any unauthorized reprint or use of this material is prohibited. No part of this book may be reproduced or transmitted in any form or by any means, electronic or mechanical, including photocopying, recording, or by any information storage and retrieval system, without express written permission from the author.

Identifiers:

Library of Congress Control Number: 2020904345

ISBN: 978-1-64746-179-9 (paperback)
ISBN: 978-1-64746-180-5 (hardback)
ISBN: 978-1-64746-181-2 (ebook)

Available in paperback, hardback, e-book, and audiobook.

Any Internet addresses (websites, blogs, etc) and telephone numbers printed in this book are offered as a resource. They are not intended in any way to be or imply an endorsement by Author Academy Elite, nor does Author Academy Elite vouch for the content of these sites and numbers for the life of this book.

Book design by JetLaunch. Cover design by Betty Martinez

DEDICATION

To the skateboard, snowboard, and ski coaches and instructors who light and nurture fires of imagination of young people around the world and show them the beauty and power of their respective sports.

To all those involved in the search, rescue, and treatment of victims of human trafficking. Trafficking is a difficult subject to cover in a short novel. I have included more information in the Author's Notes and some discussion questions at the end of the book.

And my family, of whom I am very proud:

Lindy, certified PSIA ski instructor

Jake, certified snowboard instructor, certified snowboard coach

Josh, certified PSIA ski instructor

Cameron, certified snowboard instructor, All-American snowboard competitor

ACKNOWLEDGEMENTS

Many people contributed to my care and feeding during the writing of *The Irish Skateboard Club*. Here are the biggest stars:

Jim Tritten, Ryder Beadle, Melody Costa, Scott Jones, Joseph Badal, Nathan Chismar, Michael Johnstone, Michele Magazine, Kary Oberbrunner, Nanette O'Neill, Niccie Kliegl, Abigail Young, Brenda Haire, Tony Colson, my editor Tina Molson, SouthWest Writers, Phaedra Greenwood, my Taos writers' group, my USAFA classmates, Jane Britt Vasarhelyi, and the Boquete Authors' Group.

CHAPTER ONE

JACQUE BREEDEN BUSINESS PARK
ALBUQUERQUE, NEW MEXICO

"Hey, Spider-Man, it's your turn."

"Don't call me Spider-Man. I'm not that good," Michael Anthony Callahan said.

"Dude, I saw you run straight up a ten-foot wall last week," the unofficial parkour team leader said. "It was sweet. I know a Spider-Man when I see one."

"Peter Parker is a white man, five-foot-ten. I'm five-four, 135 pounds, and sixteen years old."

"Then, you're a little brown Spidey-Mikey with a black ponytail, my man."

They stood on the roof of one of several new office complexes springing up all around Albuquerque. Michael leaned over the edge of the four-story parking garage and looked down to the parkour obstacle course that had been unofficially marked out below.

New office buildings, ramps, sidewalks, tree-lined streets, acres of concrete, boulders, and a lush landscaped park promised opportunities for a mega adrenaline rush. Nearly deserted that early Sunday morning, it was perfect for what Michael and his new friends had in mind.

He loved this sport he had recently discovered. Every parkour session was like the opening scene of a James Bond movie. Videos were popping up all over the Internet, people leaping, diving, and flipping across urban rooftops, ramps, and parks in cities from London to Tokyo. Michael called it applied gymnastics or real-world gymnastics. His father, a retired fighter pilot, would call it combat gymnastics—if he knew anything about parkour, which was doubtful. Leaping between multi-story buildings was flat-out dangerous. A simple slip or mistake could put you in the hospital—or morgue.

Michael would be the last competitor to launch, which was fine with him. He was a watcher, preferring to see what the older guys were doing, to check things out before he dove into this new situation. He was careful everywhere except on the ski slopes or in a skateboard park. Which was why he had yet to be arrested like many of his friends and why his picture hung in a place of honor on the wall of the Taos Orthopaedic Clinic. It was a Callahan family joke that Michael's snowboarding medical bills had paid for the doctor's new Mercedes.

An experienced snowboard and skateboard competitor, Michael knew the nervous tension he felt now would disappear once he started his run. This was serious stuff, exhilarating and hazardous at the same time. It was precisely what he loved and craved.

He looked down at the course destination, a circular fountain about a block and a half away, then jogged over to the opposite side of the building to prep for his run. He closed his eyes and reviewed the plan, visualizing like he would right before a run down a slopestyle course or a halfpipe. First, the leap across a fifteen-foot gap to the next rooftop, then—

Sirens shattered his concentration.

Michael jerked his head around to locate the source. Police cars were surrounding the fountain and some of the streets leading to it.

"Cops," the team leader shouted. "Get out of here!"

Perched where he was, Michael picked out the only direction away from the swarm of police, an improvised, unproven way. Not his style, but if he got caught up here, it would be jail for sure.

Relax, you can do this.

To get away, he had to leave now and fast. No time for fancy tricks. This was survival mode. Michael sprinted to the stairwell, vaulted over the wall, and dropped to the next lower level. He trotted to the other side of the building, swung his legs over a safety rail, paused to get his bearings, and leapt across the gap between the buildings. He landed hard on the sloping roof and started a semi-controlled slide down the massive air conditioning ductwork. Michael slithered to a stop across the roof. Carefully gauging the distance, he backed up, then sprinted forward, took a flying leap across another fifteen-foot gap to the next rooftop, Bond-rolled to his feet, and hurried to the other side. Two stories to go. No cops in sight.

He peered over the edge. No obvious choices. He went to another wall. Still nothing. The third wall offered a dicey option of dropping to a narrow stone ledge where two walls intersected. Normally, he would shun this if given another alternative, but the sirens sounded closer. No time, no choice. He steadied himself a moment, and over the wall he went. He hung by both hands, facing the bricks. A glance down showed at least a twenty-foot drop if he missed the ledge. He released his left hand, and his body swung 90 degrees to face outwards.

He dropped. Both feet hit the ledge at the same time. He teetered there, trying to gain his balance. The mortar on one section of the ledge gave way, and the stone slipped. He fell forward. Off balance and desperate, he twisted to get his feet under him properly and failed. He plummeted down, smashed into newly planted shrubbery, barely missed being impaled by a tree stake, and bounced. Fire lanced through his left leg, and he almost screamed. Didn't want to move ever again.

The cops!

He tried to sit up. Spasms stabbed him. He tried again. Waves of agony.

This was going to be ugly, but if he didn't get up and out of there, the cops would make it worse. He took a deep breath and rolled over. Most of the pain concentrated in his leg. He had broken enough bones in his life to know it was no sprain.

Oh God, no. I can't have a broken leg. Not now. We're supposed to go to Ireland next week. What'll I say to my dad? He's gonna kill me. Oh no, here come the cops!

He yanked off his hoodie and threw it deep into the bushes along with his cap. Reaching behind his head, he snapped the scrunchie holding his ponytail and shook out his mane of shoulder-length hair. He spotted a cluster of tools stored behind the shrubbery by the landscaping crew. Rolling toward them, he grabbed a hoe, levered himself upright, and hobbled out into full view of the arriving police.

He nearly toppled over from the pain. The hobble was the real deal.

The police car stopped. Michael's heart felt like it did too.

The officer rolled down his window. Silver aviator sunglasses framed his brown face. "*Hola, chico!* Did you see anybody run through here a few minutes ago? Blue hoodie, ball cap on backwards?"

"*No, señor,*" Michael managed to choke out. "I no see nobody like that."

The cop studied him for a moment. "You okay, *amigo?*"

"*Si, señor.* Just a cramp." He patted his leg. "I get some *agua.* Be okay soon." Michael gave a smile and a wave. *Please go away. Please go away.*

CHAPTER TWO

ALBUQUERQUE SUNPORT
ALBUQUERQUE, NEW MEXICO
THREE MONTHS LATER

Michael led his family into the cavernous airport terminal. The family, a tight group of blond giants, gathered together for Michael's big send-off for a semester in Ireland: his grandparents, aging and shrinking down toward his own five-foot-four; his father, ramrod straight like the retired colonel he was; his mother who towered over them all, her mane of blonde hair catching the sunlight pouring through the massive terminal windows; his twin brothers, Jeremy and Justin, twelve years old going-on-eighteen. Even they were taller than he was.

His grandfather put his hand on Michael's shoulder, then gently ran his knuckles along Michael's café-au-lait cheek, up through his thick hair. "How are you feeling, *Mikhail?*" he asked in Russian.

Michael slid his arm around the waist of the old man who had spent over 30 years in Russian jails and insisted on speaking the language with all his grandchildren. He was the only person in the family to call Michael something other than the hated nickname, Mikey. Michael replied in Russian, "A little nervous, *Dyedushka*"—Grandfather. Michael had never been to Ireland. The Callahans had taken a family trip there in late spring, which he had missed because of his broken leg—another major sore point with his father. Michael had lost that opportunity; he was determined not to blow this one. He flashed a quick smile. "But I wanted this trip, and nothing's gonna stop me now."

One way or another, after this semester abroad, Michael knew life would never be the same again. Maybe better, maybe not. It was a big-time gamble on his part. In his hometown of Taos, he had it made. There, he was surrounded by Native Americans and Hispanics who looked like him, lots of friends, and his influential and well-known adopted family. He had his own status as a jock and an honor student. In Ireland, he would be merely another foreigner in a land dominated by pale-skinned people with light colored hair, people who would not, could not, know him in the same way as those he was leaving behind.

It might not be his last chance to immerse himself in Irish culture, to learn how he might find his place in this family of proud Irish-Americans, but he wanted the answer right now. Michael couldn't wait to get away and re-invent himself, starting with his name. He was a teenager, convulsed by hormones, searching for his own identity. Patience was not in his vocabulary.

The middle-aged couple clogging the first-class line was finally ticketed and their mountain of luggage processed. The overworked American Airlines representative looked at Michael, smiled, and beckoned him closer. His twin brothers swarmed forward and pushed his luggage toward the counter. Michael picked up his skateboard and the tube containing his fly rods, the most precious things he owned, and his backpack with all his electronics, the most expensive things he owned.

Boy, is this lady ever going to be surprised. She probably thinks I'm this family's gardener or something. Won't she be stunned when I hand her my itinerary to Ireland, where everybody would look like the family I'm leaving?

"Passport, please."

Michael took a deep breath. This was it, his Rubicon. There would be no going back after this. He slid his passport across the counter.

"Purpose of your trip?"

"I'm going to be an exchange student in Ireland."

"Ooh, how exciting." Her face lit up. "I imagine living there will certainly be different from New Mexico."

He pulled himself up to his full stature, such as it was. "I am returning to the land of my family ancestors."

Her smile took on a look of uncertainty as she studied his passport, which proclaimed him a full-fledged American citizen with his birthplace listed as Bolivia. Apparently, not many Bolivian-born, brown-skinned, black-haired leprechauns passed through Albuquerque bound for Ireland to rejoin their ancestors. Recovering her composure, the agent punched the computer keyboard and cranked out reams of paper. Then, she tagged his bags and handed him back his boarding pass, passport, and baggage claim tags.

"Everything is fine, young man. Enjoy your flight."

As he thanked her and turned away, a loud youthful voice rang out. "*Oye*, Miguel!" Michael turned to see a tall (to him) figure dressed in full cowboy gear loping down the wide hallway. The boy slid to a stop in front of Michael. "You can't leave without saying *adios* to me, bro."

Fabian Hernandez was his best friend, a proud Native American from the Taos Pueblo. Almost as tall as Michael's dad, Fabian's skin was several shades darker than Michael's, burnished from long hours in the saddle, raising horses and running cattle on his family's small ranch adjacent to the Pueblo lands. The two teenagers could pass as brothers, though brothers with very different tastes. Fabian wore a cowboy hat and boots, dusty Levi's, and western-style shirt; Michael had long hair and was decked out like the rabid skater he was in baggy shorts, a Dead Pawn Skateboards T-shirt, Vans shoes, and a baseball cap worn backwards.

Laughing, the boys chest-bumped. Fabian doffed his hat and faced the Callahans. "Good afternoon, ladies, General Callahan, Colonel Callahan." He pretended to whack the twins on the head with his hat. "Hey, little dudes."

"Hello, Fabian," said Michael's mother as she hugged him. "This is a lovely surprise. Thank you for coming."

"No problem, *Señora*. Me and my uncles are over at the fairgrounds buying some horses to break. They said I could come see Miguel before he left us. I Uber'ed over. Gotta be back pretty soon, though."

He turned back to Michael. "Wish I could go with you, man."

"Me too."

Fabian's family needed his skills on their ranch. A trip to Albuquerque, almost a three-hour drive south from Taos, was a big deal in the Hernandez family. Flying off to Europe was not even a fantasy.

With a sly glance toward the adults, Fabian switched to *Tiwa*, the language of the Taos Pueblo Indians. "Let me know about those Irish girls, bro. The ones I seen on the Internet look pretty hot."

"Dude, I'm not going to Ireland to check out the girls. I'm trying to learn the Irish culture."

"Aren't girls part of the culture?"

Even Fabian, his best friend, didn't get it. Michael wasn't going to Ireland to check out the babes. He was trying to see if he could squeeze some Irish-ness into his mocha skin wrapper so he could be a better Callahan.

The group made its slow passage through the jumbled stream of people going out toward Departures and passing those coming in from Arrivals. The twins dashed ahead to the escalators, ran up, then back down to join the bubble of Callahans and Fabian. Each of the adults maneuvered within the group to get one last pre-departure touch with Michael. He felt his *dyedushka* slide his hand into a pocket. Michael smiled to himself—he was now 50 dollars richer. Before each family trip, his grandfather always slipped each of the boys a brand-new 50-dollar bill to spend on anything he wanted.

His *babushka*—grandmother—put her arm around his shoulders and whispered goodbye. His father reached over and twisted the bill of Michael's hat to the front and gave a little smile.

"Make the most of this trip, kiddo."

Michael wondered how much his family would miss him. Nobody was listening to his dreams; nobody—except Fabian—was paying any attention to his words and actions. *I want to be a snowboard coach. They want me to go to college. I want to be outdoors on the mountains. They want me to get a job in a company. I don't fit in this family. They just don't get me. It sucks to be me.* He was sure that life was so good for the others in his family that nobody would even notice when he left.

When they reached Security, Michael didn't know how to say goodbye to everybody. His mother fixed that.

She threw her arms around him and lifted him off the ground. She whispered, "I can't believe my baby's going away for almost five months."

Her hair covered his face like a soft blanket, and he let himself go limp in her arms. He loved the way she held him, her special scent.

"Jeez, Mom!"

She squeezed him harder, then let him down, wiped her eyes, and smiled. "I know, luv. I just hope you find what you're looking for."

"Mom, it's going to be fine."

Suddenly, he felt totally alone. He tried to ignore the sinking feeling in his stomach and forced a smile. Time to go. He kissed his mother and grandparents, fist bumped the twins and Fabian, shook hands with his father, and walked down the ramp into Security, wondering if this adventure would make him into the Callahan he so desperately wanted to be.

CHAPTER THREE

AA FLIGHT 3513
O'HARE INTERNATIONAL AIRPORT
CHICAGO

Michael peered out the window as his aircraft taxied through the rain lashing the tarmac. Still emotionally wired with pre-departure adrenaline, he had passed the bumpy flight watching movies on his iPad. The aircraft was almost ten minutes early into Chicago, which would make his next move a bit easier. He had one task he had assigned himself despite less than a two-hour connection for his international flight.

He was forced to shuffle through the tight-packed crowds bustling along the corridors, inevitably clustered at random in the most inconvenient places, until he found the elevated monorail and zipped over to Terminal Two. He trotted down the concourse, dodging electric carts and clueless passengers glued to their cell phones.

Michael found his grandfather's favorite place in O'Hare, a wide spot in the corridor dominated by a shiny World War II U.S. Navy fighter. He turned his phone back on as he passed the display, backed up to the plane, and took a selfie. Too close. He approached a gray-haired older man wearing a suit with a badge that proclaimed him as "Timothy Simmons, DDS, Docent."

"Sir, could you please take my picture next to the airplane?"

With a smile, Simmons took his phone and motioned Michael over. "You're backlit standing near the windows." He lined up the shot, then handed the phone back. "There you go."

"Thank you. I'm going to text this to my grandfather."

"I'm here to answer any questions tourists have about the display," Simmons said. "Do you know anything about this airplane?"

Michael nodded. "It's an F4F Grumman Wildcat. It's painted just like the one Butch O'Hare piloted on the day he saved the USS Lexington from attack by nine Japanese Mitsubishi bombers. He was awarded the Medal of Honor."

Simmons smiled again. "Pretty impressive, young man. Most passengers who come through here have no idea who the airport is named after. Or what he did."

"Butch O'Hare is one of my grandfather's personal heroes. He asked me to pass on his respects."

"Really?"

"My grandfather's my own personal hero. He was a fighter pilot. So was his father. And my father. Great-Granddad actually met Commander O'Hare in the Pacific during the war."

The docent looked impressed. "Not many young people know much about World War II, young man."

"Every kid in Taos knows, thanks to my grandfather. He's a retired major general. Every Veterans Day, he wears his uniform to the high school and talks about American history. He's pretty classy—he's like a grandpa to the whole town. And lots of the kids come from the Pueblo so we know about the Navajo Code Talkers who came mostly from Arizona and New Mexico."

"Sounds like Taos is a good place to grow up."

"It is." Michael felt the first pangs of what could only be homesickness welling up in his gut. He fought them down. *I gotta do this trip.*

As he rode the monorail back to the international terminal, he used his phone to check Irish weather. Stormy and rain in Dublin, just like this afternoon in Chicago. Not good. He needed to get used to the idea of so much rain.

The area surrounding the counter at his gate was jammed, and the standby board listed nearly a dozen names. A freckle-faced boy with longish hair about his own age sat off to one side in a wheelchair, arm in a sling and a leg in a cast. He was dressed much like Michael—baggy shorts, a mountain bike jersey, and cap worn backwards. He had an anxious look on his face.

Michael slid over and said, "Dude, what happened? Wait, don't tell me—skateboard or mountain bike?"

The kid looked up and said with a wry smile, "Mountain bike. I trashed myself big time."

"Been there, buddy. Over the handlebars?"

"Yep."

Michael chuckled. "Been there too. Physics strikes again. I broke my wrist and my arm snowboarding. Last May, I broke my leg."

"How about mountain biking? Anything broken there?"

"Nah, just bruises so far. Maybe next year." They both laughed. "I'm Michael."

They shook hands. "I'm Max Ewen. I've been with my grandparents in California. Missed my scheduled flights because of the accident. Gotta meet my parents in Rome tomorrow."

"You live there?"

Max nodded. "My parents work in the U.S. Embassy."

"*Si? Come ti piace l'Italia?*" —Yeah? How are you enjoying Italy?—Michael said.

"Love it," replied Max, also in Italian. "I've been at the International School in Rome for two years now. It's great."

"My grandmother grew up in Siena," Michael said. "I've been there a lot. We speak Italian in her house back in New Mexico."

There was another incoherent announcement over the airport loudspeaker about their flight.

Max made a fist with his good hand and banged the wheelchair armrest. "I just have to get on this flight! Chicago to Dublin. Dublin to Vienna. Vienna to Rome. But I gotta get to Dublin first! This is my only chance to connect today!"

"Long way to go to get home, dude."

"Too true. Thirty hours start to finish."

The gate attendant hurried through the crowd to hand Max a boarding pass. "You can board now. We found you a seat near the rear. Sorry, but that's the best we can do. The plane is completely full."

Michael looked down at Max and tried to imagine how awful the flight would feel, stuffed in a rear seat, people bumping into his leg on their way to the toilet. Brutal.

He showed his ticket packet to the attendant. "Give him my first-class seat, please. I'll ride in back."

Startled, the attendant checked his boarding pass. "Are you sure? Once he gets seated, there's no switching over."

"I've ridden on a plane wearing a cast. It totally sucks. Even in first class. I'm small. I can fit anywhere."

As the attendant started to push the wheelchair toward the boarding ramp, Max stopped her. He dug into his backpack and produced a business card. He scribbled on the back. "This is my mom's card. She's a big deal in the embassy. And my cell number and email are on the back." He handed over the card and gave Michael a military-type salute. "Thanks, man. You're my hero. You ever get to Rome, the pizza's on me!"

CHAPTER FOUR

AMERICAN AIRLINES FLIGHT 194

The climb-out from O'Hare proved as bumpy as advertised, and the rough ride didn't stop until well after dark. Finally, the flight attendants unstrapped and started serving passengers. After dinner, Michael slipped into a dream. He was standing on a massive open grassy plateau, surrounded by snow-capped mountains. A herd of indistinct animals grazed in the distance. It was cold, and a slight breeze brought the earthy smells of the herd. He could hear someone who spoke to him in a language he felt he should understand, but it still felt foreign.

He woke up with a start and looked around. The aircraft wallowed and bounced in the rough air as it descended for landing. A drink cart broke loose and crashed into the seat behind him. Frightened voices erupted from startled passengers. The man across the aisle leaned over and yanked open the bottom drawer of the cart. He pulled out a handful of small whiskey bottles and glanced at Michael. "Here, kid, take some. If this lousy weather keeps up, we're going to need these."

"No thanks, sir. I don't drink."

"Suit yourself," said the man, then stuffed bottles into his pockets.

Michael leaned over his seatmate to get a view of the sun rising over Ireland. No airport yet. Nothing but clouds, rain, and wings flexing as the plane plowed through the weather. Finally, they broke out of the clouds over the Irish Sea. Up ahead, Ireland appeared as a green ribbon on the horizon, then grew into a multi-hued green mass as the aircraft passed over the coastline, going "feet dry," as Dyedushka would say in his pilot-speak.

Michael had two first impressions. The Irish countryside was flat. Really flat up close, with some highlands in the distance. And green! So green it appeared to glow, unlike Taos, which sat perched on a semi-arid desert mesa surrounded by shades of brown. Cultivated fields were marked by stone walls or lines of trees, water everywhere. Houses and buildings grew more common as they approached towns, then larger roads, a multi-lane highway with its sweeping curves, housing developments with cottages grouped in straight lines like marching infantry. He spotted the River Liffey as it sliced through the heart of Dublin on its way to the ocean. The Port of Dublin, the largest port in Ireland, was massive, with warehouse areas, fuel tanks, and cargo cranes spread out along both sides of the river. Ocean-going ships and ferries dotted the waterfront. Dublin itself showed lots of greenery, trees, and parks stretching for miles, no real skyscrapers or even many tall buildings in sight.

Excitement mingled with dread. Michael was an experienced international traveler, but this time he would be met by strangers, not by family. His family had petitioned the international exchange company to assign him to an active family in a small town in a rural county. Instead, he had been assigned to Dylan and Alison Jameson, childless accountants who lived in the largest city in Ireland and who spent their leisure hours gardening or playing board games. Major bummer.

After disembarking, Michael followed wide walkways with huge windows that reached from floor to ceiling and curved toward the baggage area, Immigration, and Customs. The signs were in English and what could only be the native Irish, his first encounter with that language. The airport name was displayed prominently "*Aerfort Bhaile Átha Cliath,*" which looked to Michael pretty much like a random collection of letters—with some strange letters at that. At least there were vowels, unlike some languages he had seen. Growing up in a multicultural family in a functionally bi-lingual state, Michael was pretty adept at learning languages, but Irish looked like it was going to be a whole new ballgame.

As Michael stood in line at the Immigration Control area, a uniformed man approached him and tapped him on the shoulder.

"May I see your passport, please?"

Surprised, Michael handed it over. Then stood, first on one foot, then the other as the officer leafed through it, studying each page, holding the passport up to the light to examine watermarks and entry/exit stamps. Without a word, he motioned for Michael to follow him down a corridor into a small windowless room that contained a scuffed metal table and two chairs. One wall had a large mirrored glass window like the ones featured in every cop television show Michael had ever seen. He knew it was a one-way window with people watching on the other side.

"Wait here."

"Officer, may I ask what this is all about?"

The officer ignored Michael and left. Michael sat, not knowing what was going on, but whatever it was, he knew that it was not going to be a happy beginning to his adventure.

After about twenty minutes, a different Immigration official entered the room. He was bigger and older than the first. His nametag said "Connolly." He held up Michael's passport and baggage claim tickets. "Where did you buy this passport?"

"I didn't buy it, sir. My parents and I applied for it."

"Really, now? How is it that you've been to so many places?"

"I'm lucky. I travel a lot."

"It doesn't look like a real American passport."

If it isn't real, how come I traveled so much without anyone questioning me?

The man looked Michael up and down. "You don't look American to me."

What does an American look like?

"Why, sir? Because my skin is brown? The State of New Mexico, where I live, has the highest percentage of Hispanics and the fourth highest percentage of Native Americans in the United States. They are American citizens, just as I am."

"But you weren't born in the United States, were you now?"

"No. I was born in Bolivia. My birth parents are dead. I was adopted at eight weeks and brought to the United States. Legally. I was naturalized when I was one and raised mostly in New Mexico after my father retired from the U.S. Air Force. Is that enough information to convince you that I am just a regular ole Yankee from America?"

Michael knew that one phone call to his father and his father's political connections would end this interrogation within minutes. But he would die before calling his daddy to bail him out. One of his purposes for this trip was to prove he was capable of handling himself. *Jeez, I didn't even get out of the airport! Maybe this trip wasn't such a good idea after all!*

"Look, Officer Connolly, with all the respect for you and your position that I can muster, that passport is legitimate, and I have not done anything illegal. If you don't believe me, call the American Embassy. They'll be happy to help."

Connolly stared at Michael for what seemed like an hour.

This guy is ice-cold. Lucky for me, I'm innocent!

A knock on the window. Without a word, Connolly stood and left the room.

Ten minutes passed. *I sure hope someone comes soon and clears me. My host parents may think I missed the plane and leave me here.*

A different man slipped in. He had more badges on his uniform, gray hair, glasses, and an air of authority. Probably a senior official.

He piled Michael's backpack, fly rod tube, skateboard, and baggage claim tickets on the table, then sat. "I am Superintendent Buchanan. You've done quite a bit of travel for such a young lad."

"And I never had a problem with my passport, sir."

"Actually, young man, all that travel to some pretty exotic places is exactly what caught the eye of our officials." He chuckled. "That and the skateboard."

And probably the long hair. Next trip, I shove it up under my cap. "Sir, my family has properties all over. My grandmother is descended from White Russians who settled in Italy, where she was born and raised. We visit her family home near Siena most summers. Our family visited Russia two years ago. My mother has a family ranch in Australia. My parents have friends all over Asia and Europe. We travel a bunch."

"I know. We Googled your family. Quite impressive."

"Does that mean I can go?" *Please, please let me go.*

Buchanan handed Michael his passport. He smiled and unleashed a string of words that had to be Irish.

"I'm sorry, sir. I didn't understand a word of that."

"I said you are free to go with our apologies. And welcome to Ireland. I hope you enjoy your stay."

CHAPTER FIVE

DUBLIN AIRPORT

Michael descended into the packed Arrivals corridor. Crowds of people lined the waiting area. Here and there, he saw excited groups waving and smiling, or rushing to greet a new arrival with hugs and kisses. Nobody paid any attention to him. His eyes searched the crowd and saw a thin woman holding a small placard with M. Callahan written in red. He maneuvered his baggage trolley through the crowd.

"You must be Mrs. Jameson. I'm Michael Callahan."

Mrs. Jameson stared down at him, eyes wide as she took him in from toe to head. "Oh, hello," she stammered. "I'm sorry. I thought you would be taller."

"Me too, Mrs. Jameson, but this is probably as tall as I'm going to get."

"My," she said, "you are a colorful dresser. Very casual." She tilted her eyeglasses down and looked over the rims. She was anything but colorful herself, hair drawn up into a bun, a dark skirt, plain blouse, topped with a dark sweater and what his fashion-conscious mother would call "sensible shoes."

"And why are you so late? I've been waiting ever so long."

"I'm sorry, Mrs. Jameson. There was a bit of a problem with my passport. It's all good now."

Michael sensed disapproval from this stern-looking woman. *Great, just great. You're off to a wonderful start, Michael, me boy.* He decided right then that he'd better not let her see his tattoo. She would freak. Long sleeve shirts would be his uniform around the house for the next four plus months.

He pushed the awkward luggage trolley and followed Mrs. Jameson through the automobile and bus traffic to the parking area and loaded his baggage into the trunk of her beat-up Rover.

"Mr. Jameson couldn't make it this morning but sends his regards. He had to work, you see." She eased the Rover into traffic then sped up. "We'll be taking you the long way 'round," she said. "There's been a tragedy on the motorway and the roads are blocked. The *bealach impill*—sorry, that's detour in Irish—will take us through Dublin proper."

He forced himself to focus on her speech. Her Irish lilt, while charming, was strange and difficult for him to understand.

They drove through village after village. *Wow, this is different.* Each of the towns and villages that made up the greater Dublin metroplex seemed to have its own main street lined with tightly packed shops, brightly colored two-story buildings right up to the edge of road. Lots of stone buildings, narrow streets, few of them straight, lined with trees, and tall metal streetlamps that curved over the sidewalk. Several towns boasted pedestrian streets, crowded with early-morning shoppers. Some storefronts had vegetables and fruits spilling out onto colorful display tables along the sidewalks. It was all so neat and clean. Greenery everywhere, bright flowers bursting from pots, from planters, from hedges. Churches, lots of churches, almost all Catholic. He spotted a Russian Orthodox Church—that was unexpected until he remembered from his Internet research that there was a significant and growing Russian presence in Ireland.

Even the cars were different, mostly smaller than vehicles back home in Taos. The delivery trucks were smaller as well. No Ford F-250 pickups here! But there were monster red double-decker buses.

Out of the corner of his eye, he caught a glimpse of a knot of young people ducking and weaving, disappearing, then popping back up. *A skateboard park! Yeah!*

"Mrs. Jameson, are we close to your home?"

"No, not yet. About another twenty minutes, young man."

Excited now, he settled back into his lumpy seat, a smile on his face, as they motored along. The Jameson residence was in a plain neighborhood in a long row of two-story semi-detached houses. It was the only meticulously maintained house on the street with a small fenced front yard full of flowers and neatly trimmed plants that proclaimed to all passers-by that the Jamesons spent hours in their garden.

Mrs. Jameson gave Michael a cursory tour on the way to his room. In contrast to the inside of the Callahan house, which was vibrant, big, bright, and colorful, the Jamesons' house looked like a place where nothing ever happened, and no emotions were allowed. The front room was small and decorated with wallpaper that, in Michael's opinion, did not match the carpet. Walls were covered with prints in cheap frames and photos of the Jamesons on vacation. The formal dining area looked as staged as a museum set, never used, and the entire house smelled faintly of boiled cabbage.

Mrs. Jameson showed Michael to his room, a space at the back of the house about one-third the size of his Callahan room. As he unpacked, he heard the telephone ring. Mrs. Jameson answered and spoke in low tones.

She appeared at his door. "That was Mr. Jameson. I need to go to the office. Terribly sorry. Make yourself at home. The kitchen is open to you, subject to the house rules." She handed Michael a small notebook.

Michael thought a moment. "I would like to stay awake until bedtime to reset my internal clock. I'd like to visit the skateboard park now. Could you show me how the bus system works, please?"

Mrs. Jameson sat at her desk and extracted a folder from a bottom drawer. She handed him a map from the Automobile Association (Ireland) and a well-used bus pamphlet, showed him where he would have to change busses, then departed.

CHAPTER SIX

JAMESON HOUSE
EDDINGTON

After stowing most of his clothes in the small bureau and tiny wardrobe, he checked the weather outside. Gray clouds obscured the sky and it smelled like rain. He slipped on some jeans and a long-sleeved T-shirt. He stuffed his knee and elbow pads into his backpack, then hesitated. Helmet? "Yeah, Michael," he said to himself, "you don't need to start off your Ireland trip with a concussion."

He checked his stash of euros, then grabbed his hoodie, baseball cap, and the maps, and raced out the front door and down the street to the bus stop. As he sat in the bus and watched the streets go by, his mind drifted back to the dream he had had on the flight over. The dreams were coming more often now. Not quite nightmares, not quite pleasant. Sometimes in English, sometimes in Spanish. Sometimes, like last night, in a language he felt he should know but didn't. Images he couldn't quite remember drifted through his mind the entire ride during the irregular and incessant stops made by the crowded local bus.

There were only two things Michael loved more than skateboarding: snowboarding and fly-fishing. Riding horses was up there too, maybe just a smidgen behind skateboarding. He loved watching the more urban skateboard street riders hitting stairs, grinding on handrails, skating stuff like concrete ledges and drainage tunnels. There were not many opportunities for that in Taos, but here in Dublin Towne—oh my! This semester was going to be totally epic.

The bus slowed to a stop a block from the park. Barely containing his excitement, Michael grabbed his board, rolled it out in front of him, and jumped aboard in a classic bomb drop. He pushed off and did a quick ollie over the concrete berm surrounding the park and landed inside the perimeter.

The park was gnarly—rails, stairs, rollers, a quarter-pipe and a halfpipe, and a couple ramps. There were a few younger kids, or "grommets" in skateboard-speak, and about a dozen older skaters. Dressed more or less like he was, some wore protective gear but only one wore a helmet. He watched their riding with a coach's eye. Not bad. There were a few promising riders—one boy, bigger than the others, had a few decent tricks; a couple of the girls were pretty good but none of the riders were in Michael's league. Nobody seemed to notice Michael—they were busy being enthusiastic and having fun, which was fine with him.

He promised himself he would take it easy today. His gimpy leg needed a long warm up, and he had not ridden for months. He did some slow yoga stretches, a few push-ups and some leg lifts. Satisfied, he slipped on his pads and helmet, looked around to find an empty flat area, then pushed off on his board and did some power slides, reverting from frontside to backside, then switch both ways, over and over. Then, some manuals, nose and regular. Convinced his leg would hold up, he turned back to survey the park to pick up the vibe and get the feel of the place.

This is great. Finally, back in a park. It's been too long ... way too long.

He looked for the obvious jumps and flips, and visualized his run, the line he would take, the tricks he would string together. Normally he worked on instinct, adapting as he went along. What he wanted now was to just ride. He was so amped that he could feel his heart pounding. He chuckled. *It's time, Michael, me boy!*

He took a deep breath and dropped in.

Michael felt it immediately—dozens of sensations buzzed through him. It was all automatic, yet it wasn't—it was freestyle, done by feel, judgment, and luck, every movement in slow motion. He was on today, in the zone. Drop, pump, spin, carve, frontside grab, pump, big air, kick flip to fakie. Drop back in, over and over. Riding through the burning in his leg. Ride, ride, ride. Pirouette, a backside ollie, another big air, a Japan air, then a huge air, max hang time—floating really. Back down into the bowl, all instinct now. He reveled in the freedom, the power of flight from a quick ollie to a tweaked out big air that could pop you high above the coping, totally in control. What he was born to do.

He popped out of the bowl, spotted a rail. He hadn't done a rail since the accident. *Here goes.* He slid down the rail, a frontside boardslide, then the landing. *Ouch! That hurt!* Another deep breath as he massaged his thigh. *Okay, Ace, that's enough.*

Michael rode to his backpack, shucked off his pads and helmet, and stretched. The gentle breeze cooled his skin. He felt great. As he put on his hat and turned to look back at the bowl, nobody else was riding. Scattered around the park, some of the other riders held their boards while others rested a foot on theirs. All were staring at him. It was so quiet that it was eerie. He gave a shy wave, then a thumbs-up. "Great day to ride," he said.

"Hey, dude, where are you from?" called out one kid.

"New Mexico."

The boy slapped his friend on the shoulder. "See? I told you he were Mexican." He skated closer. Some of the others followed. "I thought you were a Mexican, just like on the telly."

"New Mexico," Michael said, stressing the New, "not Mexico. New Mexico is a state of the United States of America. Like one of your counties. I am an American."

After a moment the boy said, "Oh."

Michael tried again. "We have a bumper sticker that says 'New Mexico. Not really new. Not really Mexico.'" The boy still looked confused. Still not there.

The kid's freckled face brightened. "Is it near Disney World?"

"No, it's not. Not even close, bro. Disneyland, the original one, is in California on the west coast, something like 800 miles away, almost two days of fast driving from where I live in the mountains. Disney World is on the other coast, even further."

The boy shook his head in disbelief.

Michael sighed. People in the States complained that American kids had no clue about geography. *So, geo-ignorance is worldwide.*

He said, "Maybe the best way of explaining is that compared to Ireland, the United States is out-of-control huge."

Another boy, the big kid, dressed like a serious skater with a Lib Tech T-shirt, baggy shorts, and skater shoes, shouldered his way through the knot of riders.

"What are you doing here, dude?"

"I just came to ride."

The big kid stood arms crossed, stance wide, and leaned forward to look down on Michael. "So you're a flippin' Yank. You came here to make us look bad."

Ah, the king of the park defending his position as best rider. Classic.

"You and your stupid backwards hat."

"Oh, my hat." Michael reached up and pulled the bill around. "I can wear it frontwards as well as backwards, if you prefer. I am an ambidextrous hat-wearer."

"You're a smartass hat wearer, *boyo*."

"That, too."

The kid stepped into Michael's space, face red, fists clenched. Michael could smell his breath.

Michael tensed, then fell back a half step. "Look, dude, all I want to do is ride."

"This ain't your park, Yank." The boy raised his fists.

Michael stepped back again and went into a crouch, hands up, ready for anything. The boy started to circle to his right. Michael matched the turn and locked eyes with the bigger boy. "How 'bout if I were a Mexican? Would that make any difference?"

The boy stopped, a puzzled look on his face. "What?"

"You said you don't want any 'flippin' Yanks' in the park, but what if I were an Italian? Or Bolivian? Or Australian? Would that be okay?"

"You really are a wise ass, aren't you?"

Michael smiled. "Some people may have that mistaken opinion of me, yes."

The big kid put his hands down by his sides. "You're not afraid of me, are you?"

"No."

"Why not? Most of the kids around here are."

"My mother is an aikido *sensei*. I've been doing mixed martial arts since I was five."

"So, you're not afraid of anybody."

"I'm afraid of my mother."

They both laughed.

The big kid took another step back. "I think maybe I'm going to like you, Yank. But we don't want foreigners trying to take over our park."

"Dude, sorry. I'm not trying to take over your park," Michael said. "I just got to Ireland this morning. I mean, like four hours ago. I didn't mean to start something. I just wanted to work out some of the travel kinks to help me stay awake until after dinner."

"Yeah?"

"Yeah." Michael extended his hand. "Michael Callahan at your service."

The boy hesitated, then shook it. "Nate Chismar."

Michael said, "I have a different style than you do, Nate. But we're both skaters. We love the sport."

A wary look passed over Nate's face. "Yer point, Yank?"

"We should ride together, learn from each other. I saw your switch backside 180. It was sick."

Nate smiled at the compliment. "You planning on coming back?"

Michael chuckled. "I have no idea where I am right now. It took two different buses to get me here. But yeah, I'll be back. This park is dope."

Nate laughed, anger forgotten. "You Yanks and your lingo."

"Me?" said Michael with a laugh. "I just had a thirty-minute ride from the airport with my host mother. I couldn't understand half of what she said."

CHAPTER SEVEN

WAREHOUSE
PORT OF DUBLIN

Dimitri Andropov was so excited it felt like ants were crawling under his skin as he watched his bodyguard pry open the first shipping crate. His mouth split into a wide grin, and his pulse ramped up, much as it had when he was a teenage prodigy training for the Irish rugby team. It was like the before-match adrenaline rush that he missed so much. His once finely tuned body now aging, deteriorating more each day with a knee so damaged he could hardly walk. A knee that only hurt when it rained, which in Ireland, meant he lived in almost constant pain. He leaned heavily on his cane as he limped toward the middle of the warehouse floor.

The plain wooden crates at the center of the warehouse held dozens of stolen, precious, and illegal artifacts from a land he represented but had never visited. And probably never could. His anonymity was what made this clandestine and highly profitable smuggling enterprise possible.

He slipped on a pair of nitrile gloves to protect the precious articles from handling and as a concession to his latex allergy. He was nearly giddy as he unpacked each carefully wrapped parcel. There were layers of Russian icons—religious scenes painted on wood—mostly from the 15th and 16th centuries.

"*Bozhe moy!*"—My God—he murmured in Russian, almost overcome with excitement as he examined an elaborate Madonna and Child in a gilded frame from the 15th century. He laid it on a workbench and carefully examined the surface. All the signs of antiquity were there, especially the hallmark *craquelure*, the fine cracks that laced across deep into the surface of the paint, a sure sign this icon was genuine, thus saleable. Andropov sighed, almost enraptured by the beauty of this nearly priceless piece of Russian history.

Andropov wasn't his real name, of course. Or rather, it was his real name, only not the one on his Irish birth certificate. He was born and raised in Ireland and considered himself Irish through-and-through. He had excelled at rugby with a fair chance of becoming the youngest member of the Irish national team. A savage tackle in a championship match had ruined his knee and killed his dream. He woke up in hospital the next day only to find his parents had died in a mysterious explosion on the way to the game. Reacting to his losses in typical Irish fashion, he was drunk for weeks. Eventually, his wife left him for an Argentine tennis player but not before spending all his meager inheritance.

Abandoned, broke, and desperate, he was yanked out of his drunken stupor and thrust into a country house, where he was confined by a cadre of hard-looking, serious men. Once he was sober and alert, the men swore him to secrecy and proceeded to inform him his parents had been Soviet citizens. They were trusted by their colleagues in the *Komitet gosudarstvennoy bezopasnosti*—KGB—and sent abroad, there to burrow into Irish life and wait for orders to foment discord in the West, to become what people in the intelligence world called moles. These men told him his Russian name, explained how his famous Andropov relative had been Chairman of the KGB, then General Secretary of the Communist Party. His name gave him the option to move to Russia, then emerging from the wreckage of the former Soviet Union, or to stay in Ireland—with certain conditions. He was sure there was also a third option—a bullet and an unmarked, shallow grave in the countryside should he not choose option one or two.

He had no real choice. He was penniless. And curious. So, he embraced the opportunity. He would become an agent of the Russian state while maintaining his Irish identity. They stole him a slot at Trinity College Dublin, the most prestigious university in Ireland, where he studied history and Russian. He *knew* his parents had been murdered by the American CIA, which influenced his total embrace of socialism.

This secret existence would be like heaven for him. The men who controlled him would gain. He would gain. His life was again like a rugby game except he now used his brain, not his body. If he did well for his team, he was rewarded … and the score was kept by the amount of money he collected. So far, he was well ahead.

Andropov immersed himself in the study of icons during his graduate studies and fancied himself something of an expert. Hadn't he even made the trip to the hated United States to visit the prestigious Museum of Russian Icons in Massachusetts?

He surveyed the tables now covered with the priceless icons. *This is the best shipment I've ever seen. Simply stunning.* Considered gospel in paint, icons had been venerated in Orthodox Christianity for a thousand years, carried at the head of Russian armies on the march, taken on journeys by Russian nobles for divine protection. Post-Soviet Russian Orthodox churches were now openly decorated with icons. The *narod*—people—loved them and called them *windows into heaven*.

The second crate, smaller than the first, contained jewelry. Dozens of Russian antique imperial gold brooches and stick pins, glittering diamond rings and bracelets, huge pearls mounted in elaborate settings, several rare World War I Russian Imperial Order of St. George medals. In a hand-lacquered box he found a painted enamel gold icon pendant and an original Fabergé two-color enamel egg pendant. But for him, the best was layered along the crate's bottom. Reverently, he lifted out a dozen extraordinary antiquarian books from the Russian Imperial Palace's Book collection.

As a professional historian, he itched to take one of them, any one, home. But he knew that would be his death warrant. These were uncatalogued treasures. He personally believed that many were from the world-renowned State Hermitage Museum in St. Petersburg. Reputable sources indicated that tens of thousands of items were in the basements and storage areas of the museum, unknown and forgotten over hundreds of years.

The formation of the new Russian government in the 1990s, which included many former members of the KGB, changed all that. Nothing in the old Soviet Union was secret from the KGB, or now from its successor, the *Federal'naya sluzhba bezopasnosti* (FSB).

Andropov and the world watched as Russian state assets were put up for sale and purchased by friends of the politicians, creating a new class of Russian billionaires. Some billionaires—usually referred to as oligarchs—more culturally aware and better educated than the rest, turned their eyes to the Hermitage. A combination of bribes and threats, so far discreet and undetected, created carefully controlled leaks unnoticed by the ignorant—or corrupt—authorities. A steady stream of precious items slipped out of Russia via the underground world market for art.

But now the items were property of these serious Russian businessmen who were not careless about inventory control during the shipment of the valuable cargo overseas. "Lost in shipping" was not a phrase these oligarchs tolerated. Nor would they hesitate to murder anyone who crossed them. Packing lists were meticulously scrutinized at each transshipment point.

This was what his position was for, to ensure things got where the power brokers in Russia intended for them to go. He was to arrange minimal interference from local customs officials and procedures. Being Irish, Andropov understood the country and its people better than the Russians ever could. As long as he didn't screw up, he could run the Irish market and distribute items through the small but growing Russian community in Ireland. For him, Ireland was a land of great opportunity. For his loyal service, he was floated in a sea of money.

He would allow nothing to endanger his position.

CHAPTER EIGHT

Jameson Residence

Consumed by jet lag, Michael slept the clock around. When he woke, his phone said 2 p.m. He stumbled out of bed, took a quick shower in his ridiculously tiny bathroom, dressed in shorts, a clean T-shirt, and his baseball cap, then wandered into the kitchen. Neither Jameson was home. There was a note signed by Mr. Jameson, whom he had yet to meet. "Back at 4:00. Appointment with Headmaster at 4:30. Please be prompt."

He found the thin notebook Mrs. Jameson had given him the day before. It was titled "Rules of the House," written in the precise hand of an accountant. He leafed through it. He was not the Jamesons' first student. They rented their extra room to the exchange program. Michael leafed through the notebook. No alcohol. No music after 9 p.m. Lights out at ten. No visitors of the opposite sex allowed in his room. It looked like he was locked in some sort of academic foster child program.

He fixed some eggs for a late lunch and cleaned up—as required by the rules. Restless, he went for a quick walk. The overcast skies and threat of more rain touched off a surge of homesickness. So far, he had not seen the sun since his arrival in Ireland. He missed the almost constant blue skies over Taos.

His natural curiosity at his surroundings helped distract him as he walked around. The Village of Eddington had been its own self-contained incorporated entity with its own history before it was swallowed by the urban sprawl that was Dublin. He strolled the few blocks of row houses that separated the Jamesons' from High Street, the central business district, lined with small, colorful shops and several pubs, all doing a brisk afternoon business.

Michael was back at the house five minutes early. Precisely at 4:00, Mr. Jameson, in the battered Rover, arrived.

"Good afternoon, Mr. Jameson," Michael said and stuck out his hand. "Nice to finally meet you. Thank you for hosting me."

Jameson was thin, with narrow shoulders, an indoor pallor, and a slight stoop, probably from sitting at a computer all day. His face was framed with black-rimmed glasses and his thinning hair was combed straight back. He looked Michael up and down, frowning. He said, "Too late to change, Michael. I'll see you to the appointment. It's best to be a bit early."

Michael dashed inside to grab his backpack in case the school loaded him up with textbooks along with his iPad in case the schoolbooks were online.

As they drove, Mr. Jameson gave a running account of St. George's College. "It was founded in 1669 by the Irish Catholic Church, later moved to its present location. State-of-the-art science laboratories, top-rate faculty, bloody marvelous athletics. About half the students board at the school." He paused as he made a lane change and gave Michael a look. "This is one of the finest schools in Ireland. You are a lucky lad."

"Did you attend St. George's, Mr. Jameson?"

Mr. Jameson sighed. "My parents couldn't afford it."

"How about Mrs. Jameson?"

"I should say not!" He gave a snort. "St. George's only started admitting girls five years ago. Most on scholarships, too. It's all about diversity now, isn't it?"

Welcome to the 21st century, Mr. Jameson.

Michael knew his parents were paying a bundle for this trip and this school and hoped it would measure up to Clan Callahan standards. What he saw when they drove through the gates looked more like a fancy-pants East Coast university in the States than a high school. Dominated by a massive, three-story Georgian gray stone central building covered with ivy, the campus reminded him of photos of Harvard and Princeton. The landscape was exquisitely groomed: thick rows of flowering plants that lined the drive wrapped around each of the buildings like moats, trees that wouldn't dare drop leaves on the precisely mowed lawn. Flanking the central building were modern buildings that looked like classrooms, plus extensive brick structures that were probably dormitories for the boarding students.

Yo, look at that! Surrounding the facilities were acres of athletic fields, soccer—football here—a rugby pitch, a separate cricket pitch, at least a dozen tennis courts, what looked like an indoor pool facility, a running track. *Wow! This is great. Maybe, just maybe, this trip is gonna work out!* The school was certainly not like any high school he had ever seen. The complex made Taos High look like a warehouse. Maybe St. George's wasn't quite in the Hogwarts league but still impressive.

They parked and followed signs to the administrative office. Jameson's phone rang. He turned away to take the call. When finished, he sighed and said, "Terribly sorry,

Michael. I have to go back to the office. The headmaster can give you directions on busses. Have you any euros?"

"Yes. I've got money. I'm good."

Jameson led them into the admin area. "My name is Jameson," he announced at the front desk. "I have with me a new student, Michael Callahan, here for his interview with the headmaster."

The staff stared at Michael with interest. Several spoke privately with their neighbors and giggled. Jameson and Michael were ushered in to see the headmaster.

Michael thought he looked like a headmaster should. Old, probably at least fifty, distinguished, with a full head of white hair. Blue eyes peered out from behind thick wire-rimmed glasses. Creases that lined his face added to his aura as a serious man.

"I'm sorry, Headmaster," said Jameson. "I must excuse myself. Needed at the office, you see." He turned on his heel and left.

The headmaster offered his hand, then gestured for Michael to take a seat. Michael sank into a large leather chair. "Welcome to Ireland and to St. George's College, Mr. Callahan. I trust you had a pleasant journey?"

Michael nodded. "Yes, sir. Thank you."

The headmaster said, "Excellent. Now let's get you enrolled, shall we?" He took a colored brochure from a manila folder and slid it across his oak desk to Michael. "Here you'll find some of our expectations for you and what you will experience from the college."

Michael flipped through the brochure.

"Please read the section on uniforms. Page four, I believe."

Michael felt the blood rise in his face as he read. *I forgot all about the uniforms. Nice start to your school here, Michael. No wonder all the admin people are amused.*

Michael studied the brochure. Pictures showed two boys and two girls, decked out in the informal and formal uniforms of St. George's; the boys in white shirts, college gray trousers, gray V-neck pullovers. *I mean, really, they can't do any better than gray?* There was an ugly college tie, red with dinky little crowns, and black low quarter shoes with black socks. *Oh yeah, that's classy!* The formal black blazer with the college crest was also paired with the boring white shirt.

"I assume that the uniform policy applies to everyone, Headmaster?"

The headmaster merely tilted his chin down and peered over the tops of his eyeglasses. "There are addresses of several shops on High Street where you can purchase uniforms."

"Yes, sir." *Rats.*

Michael watched the headmaster as he shuffled papers in the folder.

"I reviewed your academic transcript from Mexico. Your standardized test scores were a mystery to me—you're our first Mexican—so I emailed your principal. He had good things to say about you. Most impressive. Top marks."

"Excuse me, sir. I'm not Mexican. I'm American. From New Mexico, in the United States."

The headmaster looked surprised, then spread the papers out on his desk. He held up a copy of Michael's passport. "Dear me, so you are!" He shifted in his chair, and his cheeks took on a slight pink flush. "That explains why all the documents read so well in English. And your accent. Not at all what I expected." He shuffled the papers again. "But you do speak Spanish. It says so right here."

"Yes, sir. Lots of people speak Spanish in New Mexico."

"Quite so." He made a notation on several documents. "Now, back to the enrollment. I understand you were home-schooled for your early years."

"Yes, sir. My grandfather and I spent a lot of time together."

"To good purpose, young man. To good purpose. Consequently, we feel that you should enter our International Baccalaureate program. To stretch you a bit, you see."

He handed over another brochure. "This lists our requirements. Six courses for the term. Let's start with English. You'll take Irish literature. That covers Swift, C.S.Lewis, Shaw, Wilde, Joyce, et cetera."

Oh no, not Joyce! He's incomprehensible!

The headmaster continued. "History. You Americans," he paused, "you *Americans* have a somewhat abbreviated view of history, coming from such a young country. You'll be in the class covering the Middle Ages through Napoleon, basically European history from the year 1066 to 1815."

Michael nodded. *I have a pretty good handle on Europe from my AP World History class plus all the military stuff Dyedushka pumped into me. No problem.*

"Mathematics. I understand that you are particularly good at maths."

Michael smiled. "Thanks to my grandfather. He was a military test pilot. He thinks in equations. He drilled that into me."

The headmaster's face became even more serious. "Physics. Here at St. George's, we pride ourselves on the rigor of our science curriculum, physics in particular."

Michael smiled and nodded. *Piece of cake.*

"Microeconomics."

Michael laughed out loud.

The headmaster said, "That's the first time I've heard a student laugh about 'the dismal science.'"

"No problem, sir. I'm looking forward to taking micro." *No way I am going to tell him my mom has a doctorate in economics.*

"That's another first, young man." What could have passed for a smile flitted across his face. "Language. You are something of a linguist, I understand. We have an excellent Latin instructor who would love to get her hands on you."

Great! A snap. "I'll be delighted to meet her, Headmaster."

"Excellent, then. You'll find textbooks listed on our website. Classes nine to four in the afternoon—arrange your own transport. Many of our local students take the bus. You'll find our public transport quite dependable." He sat back in his chair and steepled his fingers. Again, he looked down over the top of his glasses. "I'm afraid, young man, that we do have a bit of a problem. He paused. "Your hair."

Oh man, I thought people were over the hair thing. If my father, the super-straight colonel, can handle long hair, anybody can. Sheesh. He sighed. *I'm gonna make this semester here work if it kills me. Anyhow, hair grows back.* "Not a problem, Headmaster. I'll get it cut before I show up on Monday."

"Excellent. The local barbers and stylists know what is required. We'll see you Monday morning. Nine sharpish. In uniform." He stood. "And Callahan?"

"Yes, sir?"

"You represent St. George's College wherever you go. We expect our students to be neat and tidy even when not in school or in uniform."

Yeah, right!

"Monday morning, Headmaster. In uniform."

"With a haircut."

CHAPTER NINE

HIGH STREET, EDDINGTON, IRELAND

Michael didn't know if the biblical Purgatory was a real place or not. If there was such a thing, he knew that for him it would consist of shopping for decades, maybe centuries, condemned to wander mindlessly in stores and malls. Shopping was a task he hoped to avoid at all costs, right up there with visits to the dentist or shoveling manure in the family stables.

His mother rejoiced at spending whole afternoons in stores. His grandmother should have an honorary doctorate in shopping. Even his younger twin brothers loved to wander malls. Only his father disliked shopping as much as Michael, but he always punted and had his wife shop for him. Michael had no such back-up team—it was all him.

He trudged through the afternoon rain the few blocks separating the Jamesons' house and High Street in search of school supplies. Michael thought about water like a kid from New Mexico. Water in New Mexico was scarce, sacred, precious, fought over. Here, water was everywhere—sloshing underfoot, streaming through the gutters, puddling and splashing in the streets, or pouring down from the skies. The Irish didn't even seem to notice.

There it was—a clothing store named "Christopher Murray, Haberdasher, Ltd." Michael took a deep breath and pushed open the door, not knowing what he expected to see but pretty sure he wouldn't like it.

Racks and racks of suits and blazers lined the store, mostly in shades of blue, gray, and black. Well, gray and black were what he was looking for so this could be the right place.

A middle-aged man appeared from behind the counter. Impeccably dressed in a light gray woolen suit complete with a vest, he wore what Michael now knew as a waistcoat in Ireland. The man eyed Michael, clearly not impressed with the baggy shorts and Vans shoes. His "may I help you?" sounded insincere.

Michael handed over the school brochure. "I need everything, sir. Two of everything. Plus shoes."

Presto-change-o! That got a big smile. "Sure, and you must be the new exchange student at St. George's! We've been waitin' for you to arrive, haven't we now? And where's me manners? I should say, *buenas tardes*! Welcome to Ireland. *Mucho gusto, señor*. And that's all the Spanish I remember from school, isn't it?" He chuckled. "Except for *cerveza*." His hearty face flushed pink. "I'm a good Irishman, am I not? I can say beer in at least six languages. And of course, there's always *baño*. Beer and toilets pretty much go together, don't they now?"

Michael didn't even bother to explain again the difference between New Mexico and Old Mexico. He only wanted to get this over with.

Two hours and three cups of tea later, Michael escaped from the store carrying several boxes of shirts, ties, shoes, and a massive credit card receipt. He'd have to return

Saturday morning for the tailored uniform trousers and blazers, followed by the afternoon hair appointment with Mrs. Jameson's stylist. (Mrs. Jameson had seemed quite relieved that Michael would have to submit to a proper haircut). The Jamesons had made it clear that they expected him to attend Mass with them. But after Mass, he was determined to go skateboarding. The weekend was not looking too bad, considering.

Now to get home in time for dinner at the local pub.

The Jamesons insisted on driving the eight blocks to their pub. Michael had read that Dublin ranked as the city with the second youngest population in Europe and was also famous for its number of pubs. It seemed that everybody in Ireland had an *our pub*.

This pub—the Jamesons' pub—known by other Irish citizens as *The Lamb and Child*, a white rambling structure with a slate roof. A shiny bronze plaque next to the black wooden door proclaimed the pub's founding in 1643. Five huge hanging baskets overflowing with bright flowers decorated the front. Inside, low ceilings with exposed wooden beams gave a feeling of intimacy. Old-style paintings, mostly hunting scenes and Irish landscapes, covered most of the available wall space. The air smelled like cooking and good savory food at that. Michael realized how hungry he was.

There was a long gleaming oak bar with a dozen highchairs and a brass foot rail, already crowded with the happy hour set, like in the movies. Two bartenders kept busy serving guests in various stages of inebriation. A three-piece band consisting of a banjo, fiddle, and accordion was finishing a set of Irish folk tunes, which, Michael thought, would take some getting used to. It was nearly as bad as listening to stoner music.

He scanned the pub's three rooms. There were a lot of diners, but it didn't feel crowded. The air was full of a babble of music, talk, and laughter. This was certainly no T.G.I.Friday's or any routine American franchise restaurant. It was free-spirited and welcoming, like many of the small cafes in and around Taos. It surprised Michael how good it felt; he was right at home.

The Jamesons spotted an empty table and threaded their way through the crowd with barely a nod at any of the other patrons. Michael was used to a more leisurely entry procession. When the Clan Callahan went to a restaurant in Taos, it amounted to more of a parade. The local veterans would invariably stand to shake the hand of his dyedushka, "The General." Michael's father, an elected county commissioner, would stop to speak to anyone with a political question. Babushka was a matriarch of the artsy-fartsy Taos artist community and was treated with plenty of hugs and kisses from locals, as was his mother. Even the three boys would invariably spot at least one of their buddies and stop for a quick fist bump. Small town living, New Mexico style.

Mr. Jameson thrust a menu at Michael and beckoned to a server. "I'll order three beers for a proper Irish toast to you, young man."

"Thanks, Mr. Jameson, but make mine a soft drink, please. I don't drink alcohol."

Jameson looked startled, like Michael had beamed down from another planet.

"Blessed me! You don't drink?"

"No, sir."

"And will you be telling me why don't you drink?"

"I just don't have the taste for it." Michael didn't want to talk about the real reason. He and his best friend, Fabian, had been at an illegal Saturday night drinking party near the rim of the Rio Grande Gorge. There was too much liquor and too many hormones and things got out of hand. While Fabian was making out with his girlfriend by the fire, his brother accidently drove his Jeep over the edge and plunged some three hundred feet to his death. It had devastated Fabian. The next morning, he had saddled his brother's big stallion and ridden into the mountains to mourn. Michael tracked him down and camped out with him for three days. Alcohol abuse had affected too many of their friends. He and Fabian pledged together to not drink, to live sober. Their mutual vow also made it easier to deal with the peer pressure to drink or do drugs.

Jameson, clearly annoyed this boy didn't seem to appreciate his national beverage, ordered the drinks and dinner while Michael settled back to soak up the atmosphere. A server emerged from the kitchen, balancing an enormous tray of food. She had a slender, athletic body but what caught his eye was the hair—a thick mass of strawberry blonde tresses plaited in a braid that reached halfway down her back. She looked about his age and moved with a high-energy efficiency. Focused on the business of delivering food, she didn't waste much time chatting up the customers. But when she did smile, it was dynamite. Many eyes followed her as she wove between tables and the kitchen.

Michael tried to keep his eyes to himself and talk with the Jamesons, but it wasn't easy. They weren't conversationalists. And his eyes kept drifting back to the redheaded girl.

Suddenly, the front door banged open and a big husky kid, probably eighteen or so, stumbled in. He leaned against the bar, unsteady. "I thought you'd still be here," he said in a loud voice toward the red-haired server. "Your shift's over, woman."

She said something Michael could not hear and turned away.

"I said, time to leave. With me." He grabbed for her. She dodged and almost dropped her tray. She steadied her grip, then slid the tray onto an empty table and faced him, hands on hips. The big kid snarled something Michael couldn't understand.

The girl pushed him away.

Infuriated, he slapped her hard across her face. She stumbled backwards into the table. Her tray crashed to the floor, bottles shattered.

He grabbed her arm and twisted, lifting her up on her toes. "I said, you'll be leavin' with me!"

The pub went quiet. Everyone fixed their eyes on their plates and pretended to ignore the confrontation. Nobody moved to help the girl.

"I'm not your woman. Leave me alone."

The Jamesons sat still as statues, eyes down.

"You're hurting me! Let go!"

He forced her toward the door.

She pulled back. "Let go of me. I'm working!"

He twisted her arm again, a mean smile on his face. Her face contorted in pain.

Michael couldn't believe what was happening. Back in Taos, every guy in the place would be lining up to take this guy down. Certainly his own father would be right there and probably his mom as well. He pushed back his chair and angled toward the bar.

"Excuse me, miss. Is this guy bothering you?"

"Mind yer own business, mate," the big kid slurred. Michael could smell the alcohol on his breath. He didn't move.

"Hey, punk! I don't think ya heard me! This is a private conversation."

"Not anymore." Michael turned to the girl, "Do you need help?"

The kid twisted her arm again. "Tell the little bugger to go away." She groaned in pain through clenched teeth.

Michael held up his hands. "You're drunk, and I'm not. Leave before somebody gets hurt. Just go."

"I'm going to mess you up, *boyo*." The kid shoved the girl away and lunged forward. Michael feinted right and went left. The kid went for the feint and crashed into the bar. Michael seized his right arm and torqued it. He slammed the palm of his left hand into the kid's armpit and bent him over. The kid tried to escape. Michael increased the pressure and drove him slowly, painfully to his knees.

"Are you ready to leave?"

The kid thrashed about in a futile effort to escape. He erupted with a string of obscenities, many of which Michael had never heard before. He had seen this level of anger, though. This guy was out of control.

Michael pushed the kid's face to the floor, then slammed his foot into his armpit. He stood and rotated the arm a bit. Another yelp of pain. More obscenities.

"I'll get you for this."

"Maybe. Maybe not. But right now, we're going to walk outside, and I'll let you go. Don't fight it, or it'll just hurt more."

Back inside, the girl was on her knees cleaning up the broken glass. Michael stooped to help. She swatted at his hands. "Go away! I didn't need your help then, and I don't need it now!"

"Sorry. I thought you were in trouble."

"Now I am, aren't I now? I'll probably lose my job because of you."

The bartender appeared, slapped the top of the bar. "Ciara, get back to work."

She shot another angry look at Michael. "I hope I never see you again." She stomped away toward the kitchen.

The bartender leaned over the bar, and in a low voice said, "I seen what you done there, lad. And I'm glad that ye did. That boy is a bad seed. Best be careful around him. You'll want to avoid him altogether, won't you now?"

Confused, Michael said, "Why didn't anybody help her?"

"Go sit and finish your dinner, lad," said the bartender, then turned away. The pub breathed again. Conversations resumed. The singer in the band started an Irish ballad.

Michael walked back to his table. Mr. and Mrs. Jameson's faces were drawn and pale.

"Do you realize what you've done?" hissed Mr. Jameson.

"I think I helped someone who was being bullied."

"That boy is the son of our méara—mayor."

"So? I don't understand, Mr. Jameson. He was hurting the girl, and nobody tried to help her."

Jameson leaned closer and hissed, "The méara is very protective. She won't like this at all, at all. You've made us targets, haven't you now?"

Michael was no stranger to local politics, with their pluses and minuses—his father was an elected official. New Mexico, a mostly rural state, was certainly not immune from small town power brokers—*patrones* in Spanish. But this was Ireland. Surely not here, too? Michael looked again at the Jamesons. Their faces registered fear mixed with more than a little anger.

Mr. Jameson threw his napkin and pushed back his chair. "We'll be leaving now."

Nobody spoke a word on the drive home. Michael sat back in the dark, his empty stomach rumbling.

CHAPTER TEN

Town of Eddington
Sunday morning

Michael watched the scenery go by as Mr. Jameson drove the battered Rover up their street, right onto High Street, through the town, and into the church car park. A sign outside the front proudly proclaimed that St. Peter's of Eddington was established in 1776. It certainly looked like Michael's idea of a Catholic church. Built with stone blocks, outside columns, a steeple towering overhead, and massive wooden front doors, the church was flanked by the requisite graveyard full of old headstones with a few newer ones scattered around.

As they entered the church, there was a muted buzz of conversation from the parishioners. One by one, heads turned and voices fell silent until those seated all stared at Michael, quietly, curiously. Michael smiled and nodded as the family made their way to their pew.

Inside, carved beams and more columns supported the high ceilings. The windows were stained glass, the higher ones clear glass for light. There were dark marble floors, wooden pews with red cushions, and a big organ with massive pipes played a soft hymn Michael recognized.

The church was beautiful in an old-fashioned sort of way, like the haunting and slightly overwhelming cathedrals Michael had visited in Europe. He liked this one.

A calm wrapped itself around him. He felt right at home for the first time since his arrival in Dublin. He was settled, had plans to meet new friends at the skateboard park that afternoon, and classes tomorrow at what looked like a fabulous new school. *I'm finally glad to be here.*

After the service, Michael made a point to shake the hand of the priest.

"Welcome, young man. It's nice to see a new face in the crowd."

"Thank you, Father. I enjoyed the service. You have a great church."

As Michael and the Jamesons stepped away from the priest, two people forced their way through the crowd, an expensively dressed middle-aged woman and a big man, wearing the black Garda uniform.

"So, Jameson, this is the troublemaker," said the woman.

Mr. Jameson went pale. "Méara, please …"

She stepped into Michael's space. His first impression of the angry face was there was too much makeup, and her hair needed some attention. But she was the mayor, and she was angry, so this wasn't going to be good.

He stepped back. "I'm sorry, ma'am, I didn't hear what you said."

She planted herself, legs wide, chin up. "You attacked my son Friday night."

What? You gotta be kidding me! Michael held up both hands, palms facing the irate woman. "Ma'am, I didn't attack anybody. Your son was hurting a young lady. I asked him to leave her alone."

She moved closer and glared into his eyes. "I don't believe you."

"He tried to jump me. I defended myself. Then, I made him leave."

"Liar! My son would never do that."

"Ma'am, there were witnesses. Mr. and Mrs. Jameson, for example." He turned to them. "Please explain to the méara what happened."

The Jamesons both stepped backwards almost like they were joined at the hip, heads bowed, eyes on the pavement. Finally, Mr. Jameson said in a whisper, "We ... uh ... we were in a different room, méara. We ... uh ... couldn't see anything."

"What?" Michael said. "You were right there!"

The big man moved in. "I'm Superintendent Hallums. You're lucky we don't arrest you for assault."

The méara's face contorted, and she ground out her words. "You interfered in a private conversation—with that Harrington slut."

"It wasn't a private conversation, ma'am. He was shouting in a pub. He was hurting her. All she wanted was to get away."

"My son is a good man." The méara slapped him. Hard.

Michael's face stung, and he felt the heat flush into his cheeks. He stepped back and took a deep breath. "He wasn't acting like a good man last night."

The priest made his way over and stepped in. "Now, now, let's have no more of these words. This is a church. Please conduct yourselves properly."

The big Garda officer ignored him. He stuck his finger into Michael's chest. "Your immigration paperwork wasn't turned in. The Garda have no record of you. You could be deported." He towered over Michael. "After this, you should be deported."

Michael bit back the words he wanted to say to this arrogant cop. Instead, he said, "The headmaster of St. George's has all my papers. They're complete, approved, and official. Sir!"

"They're not official until I say they are. Watch yourself, you little punk." He offered his arm to the méara and together they stalked off toward the limousine waiting at the curb.

Michael turned to look at the Jamesons, who were still staring at the ground. Furious, he demanded, "Why didn't you stand up for me?"

"Now, Michael, be a good lad," Mr. Jameson said in a nervous voice as he glanced at the crowd that had gathered. "Let's go home. The car's this way."

The last thing Michael wanted right now was to spend time with the Jamesons. "I'll walk home, thank you very much."

CHAPTER ELEVEN

DUBLIN

Later, as Michael rode the bus to the skateboard park, the gray sky scowled down to match his own mood. It smelled like rain, of course. It always smelled like rain.

He settled back in his seat to think. Memories of the confrontation with the méara surged up in his mind. His throat felt dry. *Why did that have to happen? Just as things were feeling good. And what is it with the Jamesons?* His chest tightened as he searched for answers, but none came. *They betrayed me. I'm glad they weren't at home when I got there. We're going to have a talk.*

The kids at the park waved as Michael rode up. "Hi, guys. Whatcha up to?"

Nate Chismar said, "I'm trying a 360 pop shove it, and can't quite get it."

"That's a really cool trick. Better than a 360 flip," Michael said. "High intermediate, I think. Want some coaching?"

Nate nodded. "Sure."

"It's all about timing and letting the board spin. Watch this. I'll go slow." Michael pushed off and did three tricks. The other kids clapped and hooted.

Michael bowed. "Thank you, thank you very much." He looked back at Nate. "Break this trick down into its components. The secret is to put the ball of your rear foot right on the tail, heel out. Grip the tail with your toes, then pop straight down hard. That'll make the board spin flat." He demonstrated the proper placement of his rear foot.

Nate tried. The board clattered on the concrete. He tried again. Same result.

"Almost there, bro. Try to get moving forward a little and scoop it really hard. Like this." Michael demonstrated again and did three in a row. Murmurs of approval. "You're almost there, Nate. Try again. Set your rear foot. Pop straight down hard. That's the secret." Michael showed him again.

Nate rolled forward. Popped. The board clattered on the concrete. He tried again and stuck it. By this time, everyone at the skate park was watching and cheered him on.

"Try again," Michael said.

Nate popped again, then again, and again. Three in a row.

He rolled up to Michael and fist bumped. "Thanks. You're a pretty good teacher."

Pleased, Michael said, "Thanks. I want to be a professional coach someday."

Before anyone else could try, thunder rolled in and it started to pour.

Everybody grabbed their backpacks. "Follow us, Michael," shouted Nate. They scampered down the road and into an alley, then downstairs into a basement. Everybody relaxed, threw their packs on some benches and sat. "This is where we hang when it's raining. Or if we have to hide from the coppers." Nate smiled a Mona Lisa smile. "Have you ever had to run from the coppers, Michael me boy?"

Michael hesitated. "Twice."

"Twice? My goodness. You're almost a pro, dude. What happened?"

"Once in Albuquerque I was riding in the concrete drainage ditches. They're like halfpipes but massive. And posted 'No Trespassing.' The cops came, sirens and all. We scattered. I was lucky."

"And the second time?"

"I was in a new office complex and about to run a parkour course when the cops showed up. I got away but broke my leg. Pretty gnarly."

"Oh my, you are a naughty boy."

"Skateboarding isn't a crime, you know."

"Yeah, I know, you know, and we know, but the coppers don't."

Still smiling, Nate looked around the room. "I'm not sure that honest, law-abiding citizens like us should be associating with criminals, now should we, lads?"

The boys laughed. Several made profane but good-natured comments. Nate reached over and offered his hand. "Welcome to Ireland."

When the lads had finished teasing, Nate said, "Want to see something pretty cool?"

Relieved, Michael said, "Sure."

Nate pulled a flashlight—or what Michael now knew as a torch in Ireland—out of his backpack, walked over to a wooden cabinet, and opened the doors. "Follow me."

"What's this, something out of Narnia? Where are we going?"

Michael followed Nate through the cabinet and down another, hidden, flight of rickety stairs. "See for yourself. We don't show this to just anybody."

Nate aimed his torch through the opening and illuminated a tunnel, dirty brick arches stretching into the blackness.

"Dude!" Michael said.

"There are tunnels all over Dublin, all over Ireland for that matter," Nate said. "There's lots of tunnels here, some big, some little." He chuckled. "There's even a guided tour now around the Dublin Castle and the City Center underground and a couple YouTube films showing some of the tunnels. This tunnel is blocked by the City at one opening. Me da found this opening when he was a lad. The City don't know about it."

"Where does it go?"

"Pretty far. One of the branches goes toward the city center. Another snakes over toward the wharfs."

Michael said, "I've been in caves and some massive caverns in New Mexico but nothing like this—tunnels under a city. Dude, this is sick."

"What?"

"Cool … it's very cool, mega cool."

Nate laughed. "You Yanks."

"I wish I could stay and explore, but I have to get back," Michael said. "Do a little dinner, a little preview of my classes, try on my uniforms. You know, school stuff."

"You aren't one of them boarding students at that fancy pants college now are ya?"

"No, I live with a family."

"Good. Most of them boarding students are real upper-class pricks."

CHAPTER TWELVE

Port of Dublin

Dmitri Andropov sat in his office waiting for his men to bring his latest guest in for a chat. It would be a short one. He shifted in his chair to make his injured leg more comfortable but could never get far from the pain. The excruciating hammering in his knee was always there, waiting to ambush him if he ever relaxed.

He heard the delivery door hum, cars doors slam, then angry voices as his Russian assistants marched their captive into the warehouse. He had created the routine—they deliberately allowed their prisoner to see the outside of Andropov's place of business, an apparently dilapidated warehouse on the edge of the Port of Dublin, then they walked him through the cavernous interior. Inside, it was meticulously clean, with state-of-the-art heating and cooling, security systems, and an enormous vault where he kept the particularly valuable jewelry. He designed the route to show prospective customers the extent of the inventory he controlled. Brilliant Russian icons were laid out in an orderly fashion, some still in their original shipping crates, others repackaged for delivery to clients. It was a smooth, efficient system. Impressive and secure.

His assistants entered the massive office leading the nervous-looking man. The man's eyes focused on Andropov, which was disappointing. Unfortunate that the man, one Garrett Hooker, did not seem to appreciate his surroundings.

Perhaps it was because he knew he was about to die.

Still, he should appreciate beauty. Andropov felt particularly proud of his office. People had died so he could furnish this office like he was a tsar. Icons of various sizes lined one wall, their gilt paint adding light and a sense of opulence to the office. A 16th century Persian rug covered the floor and a medieval tapestry decorated the wall behind Andropov's workspace. Another carpet was temporarily missing due to a particularly troublesome bloodstain.

His desk was a massive stone table originally made for the Medici family who ruled Florence for three centuries. A 17th century spectacular example of *pietre dure,* it was a single slab of white marble inlaid with semi-precious stones—jaspers, agates, carnelians, and lapis lazuli—to form intricate multi-colored geometric designs and flowers. It had taken over fifty years to create. Would probably rake in two million euros at Sotheby's if he could only bear to part with it. He liked to imagine that Lorenzo the Magnificent, the wealthiest man from Europe's wealthiest family, once sat at a table much like this one.

Andropov did most of his work anonymously, using the Dark Net, the underbelly of the Internet, and clandestine contacts. He met only carefully selected, wealthy foreign clients face-to-face. He used the office to impress them with his ability to obtain museum quality, nearly priceless items. It usually worked: the sheer sumptuousness of the surroundings aided in his negotiations, intimidating buyers who waffled at paying his high prices and stifling their arguments. This was Hooker's first, and last, visit to the premises.

Face covered with sweat, Hooker huffed, "Mr. Andropov, why am I here? Why I am being treated this way?"

Andropov gestured to one of his men, who stepped over to a gold antique Russian samovar perched on a side table. He poured a glass of tea, added one heaping teaspoon of sugar, placed the glass in front of his boss, then stepped back next to Hooker.

Everybody waited as Andropov slowly stirred his tea.

"We've done business before," blurted Hooker. "Is this any way to treat a loyal customer?" He extended his hands like one of Andropov's iconic saints.

"Customer, yes, Garrett. Loyal, I'm not so sure." *He's such a krest'yanin—peasant!*

"What the devil do you mean?"

"I am disappointed with you, Garrett."

"I think there must be some mistake, sir."

Not a very convincing liar. "Yes, there has been a mistake. Yours. I understand that you've been selling fake icons and representing them as being from my stock."

"Oh God, let me explain. Please." Beads of sweat formed on his forehead. "That wasn't me."

"Really?"

"That wasn't me!" said Hooker in a shaky voice. "It was Mahoney! He's a runaway train, always doin' things I didn't tell him!"

"It seems unlikely to me that your top man would do something like that without your knowledge." He gestured toward his own men. "They wouldn't." *They may be nekul'turniy—uncultured—as well as stupid, but not that stupid.*

"I don't know why he did it. I had nothing, nothing to do with it. I swear to you on the heads of my children."

This is tiresome. Andropov nodded at one of the Russians who placed a cell phone on the table and tapped the screen. A scream pierced the air.

"Perhaps you recognize that voice as your associate, Mr. Mahoney, in this recording?"

Words poured out of the speaker. "It was Hooker's idea. He said we could make a lot of money quick, then disappear." A scream. "Please don't. I swear it's true!"

Andropov took a sip of his tea. "There seems to be a lot of swearing in your organization, Hooker."

"He's lying. You have to believe me!" Hooker slid out of his chair onto his knees. "Please, please, Mr. Andropov. I have a family!"

Can't you even die with dignity? Andropov shook his head. "You see, Garrett, actions of this kind simply can't be ignored. It's bad for business."

He turned to his men and said in Russian, "Another little accident, my friends. Do it tonight."

His men dragged Hooker out of the room, his futile pleas for mercy echoing in the warehouse.

Andropov tilted his head to the side and regarded the only decoration on his polished stone desk, a carved teak pipe holder inlaid with ivory, and retrieved his favorite antique Meerschaum. He carefully loaded the intricately carved pipe with his special tobacco blend and lit it with a heavy, solid-gold lighter. After several draws, he reached into a desk drawer for an exquisite, well-worn leather-bound first edition of Chekhov short stories. He opened it to a particular favorite, *The Death of a Government Clerk*, and began to read.

CHAPTER THIRTEEN

Eddington

On the bus back to the Jamesons' house, Michael sat with his skateboard across his lap and stretched. He was surprised at how much better he felt after riding with his friends. *I've got some new buds at the park. Sounds like my classes are going to be interesting. I'll meet some kids at school this week.* He grinned to himself. *I'm back on track. All I have to do now is to make peace with the Jamesons.* He settled into his seat, a smile on his face. *Yeah, I've got this.*

The rain had stopped, at least for now. Michael smiled to himself about placing the biblical tale of forty days of rain in Ireland. Perhaps Noah was Irish, he mused—forty days and forty nights of rain was not just possible in Ireland, it was probable and almost even normal.

He walked home from the bus stop, turned the corner onto the Jamesons' street, and slammed to a halt. He couldn't believe what he was seeing. Mr. and Mrs. Jameson stood on the small front porch with all of his suitcases and the boxes with his new school uniforms!

That's my stuff! He broke into a run. "What's going on?" he shouted as he hopped the fence.

Mr. Jameson said, "You cannot stay here." His voice was cold and emotionless.

"What? Why?"

"It's been decided. You cannot stay here any longer. You are a liability."

"But, but ... who decided that?" Michael's brain was frozen. *This can't be happening!* "You contracted to keep me for the term! You can't just kick me out."

"We've called the college. Someone will come to collect you."

Stunned into silence, Michael just stared at the Jamesons. *This isn't right!*

A black Range Rover pulled up in front of the Jamesons' house, and the headmaster got out, dressed in casual clothes and looking not at all friendly as he stalked up the sidewalk.

"Are these all your things, Mr. Callahan?"

"I think so, Headmaster. But—"

The headmaster waved him quiet. "Go through your former room to make sure everything is accounted for."

"But—"

"Please."

"Yes, sir." *What am I going to do now?*

Michael searched his room and went back outside. "Nothing left behind, sir."

"The check, Jameson," said the headmaster.

Jameson hesitated.

"The check, Jameson," said the headmaster, steaming.

Mr. Jameson disappeared into the house. When he returned, he carried a check and, without a word, handed it over.

The headmaster studied it. "This is what the Callahan family paid you to care for Michael?"

"Well," stammered Mr. Jameson, "I deducted the cost of his three nights. And his meals. Plus the dinner at the pub."

The headmaster shook his head. "This is exactly what I would expect from you, Jameson." He started to pick up a suitcase but straightened up and looked Jameson in the eye. "There's a good reason you weren't accepted at St. George's, Jameson. I know you tell people it was because your parents couldn't afford the tuition. The reason you were rejected had nothing to do with economics. It was all about character. In your case, the lack thereof."

He looked down at Michael. "Come on, lad. Let me give you a hand."

It took two trips to load Michael's belongings. The Jamesons made no effort to help.

The headmaster got in, banged the door shut, and sped out of the neighborhood toward the college.

"On the way over," he said, "I visited the Lamb and Child pub and spoke with the bartender. He was quite complimentary about you. Said you are a courageous young man."

"I'm not courageous, Headmaster. I just did what anyone would have done."

"Apparently not. Jameson was there and didn't do a thing."

"Okay. *Should* have done."

"Quite right."

Michael paused. "Headmaster, I hope helping me won't get you in trouble with the méara."

The headmaster gave Michael a quick glance. "Thank you, young man, but don't worry about me. Or her. I'll not have her interfering with the running of this college. Not while I'm headmaster." He turned into the entrance for the school.

"You'll board here. We have a spare room. I'll let your parents know that this was the best solution. The Jamesons were not suitable for you."

Michael followed him into the building, up some stairs, and into a well-appointed room at the opposite end of the building. The room was tidy with a bed, a desk, built-in bookshelves, and a wall closet. Not very personal but not too bad, considering. Certainly better than his room at the Jamesons.

Michael threw what he was carrying on the bed and sat, shoulders slumped.

The headmaster placed the suitcases near the closet, then leaned against the desk and folded his arms. "Michael, I want you to know that you did nothing wrong."

"Sure feels like it." Michael looked up at the headmaster. "This is messed up."

"Again, son, you did nothing wrong."

"Then, why am I here? I'm not supposed to be in a boarding school," he nearly shouted. He clenched and unclenched his fists. Then, he stopped. His gaze shifted to the floor and his shoulders slumped again. In a soft voice, he said, "I'm supposed to be with an Irish family. That's all I wanted."

"During our interview, you told me that you wanted to learn about the Irish culture. Correct?"

Michael didn't answer. He was too busy fighting back tears.

"Michael, look at me. Am I correct?"

A pause. "Yes, sir."

"We Irish are quite proud of our culture. But we, like every other culture, every other people, every other country, organization or group of humans, sometime fall short of perfection. This is one of those times."

"I sure fall short of perfection," Michael said, bitterness in his throat. "Perfection's not even on the horizon." He looked up to face the headmaster. "Mr. Jameson said that the méara's going to get me thrown out of the country."

"Don't worry about that. Your student visa and immigration papers were properly filed, despite what her husband told you." The headmaster stood up. "You'll get your chance to learn Irish culture here at the college. We like to think of ourselves as a family. You became one of us as soon as you enrolled. Under the circumstances, this is the best place for you right now." He glanced at his watch. "Get yourself cleaned up. Dinner will be served in thirty minutes. You'll take your meals in the college cafeteria." He laid his hand on Michael's shoulder and smiled. "Give this some time to settle down, son. I'll see you tomorrow."

Dinner was a disaster. The food was okay, some strange items he didn't feel like dealing with. He was ignored by the other kids—some family! It was about what he expected. And tonight, he really didn't mind. His emotions had been roller-coasting all day and he was mentally exhausted.

Back in the room, Michael unpacked, connected to the Internet, set up his school accounts, and scrolled idly through his textbooks to kill some time until well after dark. *Of course, the Jamesons caved. They're scared. The Garda has influence. The méara has influence. The Jamesons could lose business. They're not exactly prosperous. Wonder what she said to induce them to give me up along with my payment? Musta been pretty hardcore.*

Inventing excuses for the Jamesons didn't make him feel any better. He muttered, "So, I've been here less than a week and I've gotten into a fight, been shaken down by the cops, and fired by my host parents. All because I defended that redhead who never wants to see me again. Now I live in a barracks. Good work, Michael. Nice going. Your family will be thrilled to hear of your exploits. Won't they be proud!"

He sat and stared at the wall. Tears welled up in his eyes. Normally, when he was bummed, he logged into the Internet and vanished into cyberspace. Not tonight. He turned out the lights, sat in the darkness, the room as black as his spirit. His stomach ached. How was he going to explain this to Dyedushka, probably his biggest fan? His mother wouldn't say anything, nor would Babushka, but he knew they would be beyond disappointed. And his father, the super achiever, wouldn't even begin to understand.

Michael curled up on his side. There was no way this was going to turn out good.

CHAPTER FOURTEEN

CAFETERIA,
ST. GEORGE'S COLLEGE

Michael made his way through the cafeteria breakfast line, nodding occasionally to other boys. Overcome by shyness, he headed to a table as far from the others as he could. His subconscious must have worked overtime while he slept. A night's sleep and a long hot shower in the communal bathroom helped him feel almost human again. His battered ego was still bruised, but at least now he felt optimistic there was nothing else nasty and horrible out there to grab him. Anyhow, he really had no choice but to "soldier on" like Dyedushka would say. His only other option was to run home to Taos, and he could never accept that. He had to believe the worst was over.

Michael scowled down in wonder at the amount of food that sat like a future gut-bomb on his plate. An Irish fry-up of eggs fried in grease, bread fried in grease, tomatoes fried in grease, sausage, black and white pudding, baked beans, and toast. The only thing that smelled good was the cup of tea. *Oh well, I wanted to learn about the culture.*

"It's you again!"

Startled, Michael looked up. Right in front of him was a red-haired lioness, nostrils flared, and red-in-the-face. The server from the pub.

Oops.

Michael jumped up and tried to smile.

"What did you think you were doin', interferrin' in me life? Did I ask for help, *boyo*?"

"I thought you were in trouble."

"Why?" She stepped into his personal space. She had the most wonderful eyes, even though they were boring holes through him. "Because I'm just a girl? Is that what you thought? That I needed some … " She looked him up and down. "Some undersized knight to ride to my rescue?"

"No, not really," he said, drawing out the words. "Not exactly. All I saw was a bully picking on someone."

Ah. That stopped her.

"You look like an athlete," he said. "A gymnast maybe. Or a dancer. You can probably take care of yourself. I was just focused on the bully. I hate bullies."

She paused and slid back a bit. "Me, too. He is a bully, isn't he now?" Then, she smiled, and her face came alive with something like curiosity but still tempered with skepticism. "My name's Ciara. Ciara Harrington."

He extended his hand. "Keira, like the movie star, Keira Knightly?"

She gave him a look. "Yes, pronounced the same, but I spell it the Irish way, starting with a C." She spelled out her name for him. "And I'm not a dancer now, am I? I was a gymnast, though. What's your name?"

"Michael Callahan."

She looked startled. "Callahan? Our new foreign student is a Mexican named Callahan?"

Again with the Mexican? "It's Michael Anthony Callahan, and I'm from the United States, not Mexico. *New* Mexico. An American state."

She laughed. "And hasn't the school been bubbling over with the idea of a Mexican all weekend long? We've never had a Mexican here before in the entire history of the college."

She shook his hand. Hers was as smooth as her blue eyes were totally gorgeous. This was not a soft hand. Just smooth.

"Sorry to disappoint you," he said.

"Oh, I'm not disappointed, am I? You're still exotic. One-of-a-kind, I suspect."

Michael looked around the cafeteria, crowded with students for breakfast. He *was* exotic. Or more accurately, different. In a sea of mostly Irish white kids with light hair and creamy complexions that seemed to glow, he knew he stood out with his thick black hair, dark eyes. And of course, he was short. Even the kids with dark hair had rosy variations on the creamy skin, while his skin was colored like a cup of chai, or since he was in Ireland, a cup of tea—Darjeeling or Earl Grey.

She was tall—at least to him. Probably five-foot-six or seven. Her body was muscled and she walked with the grace of a model—confident, head up, shoulders back. The strawberry-blonde hair was simply perfect. He studied her face. She was criminally hot. Not a classic beauty like his adoptive mother. Not *Cosmo* or *Vogue* hot. But real. Real and hot. Fierce. Strong. Someone who would look great on the cover of *Snowboarder Magazine*. She even made the ugly school uniform look good.

"You're here early, Michael Callahan. How did you get to school today?"

"I didn't have to do much. Just walk down some stairs and a couple hallways. I am now a boarding student."

Surprised, she asked, "You mean the Jamesons threw you out?"

"Yep. On the street. Literally."

"Why ever would they do that?"

"Because of what happened at the pub. The méara and her husband made a big deal out of it."

"Oh, Michael." She reached out and touched his arm. "I'm so sorry to have been a part of that trouble."

He waved off the apology. "Not your fault."

"What did you do then?"

"I didn't have much time to think. The headmaster drove up. He was smoked.

"He told Mr. Jameson that the reason he wasn't accepted at St. George's was because of his character. Or as he put it, 'lack thereof.'"

She nodded. "And isn't he right? Character is the most important aspect of a person." She slid her books onto a chair. "I'll be getting some breakfast now. Be right back."

His spirits soared as he watched her stride away. Things were looking up this morning.

She returned quickly with a tray that contained more food than his own crowded plate. She noticed his incredulous face.

"I'm on scholarship, and doesn't it include breakfast and lunch? I eat as much as I can at school. That way me ma doesn't have to feed me. Just me little brother. I'm a scholarship baby; you're a boarder. I'm on the wrong end of the class system here, boyo."

"Why is that?"

"We scholarship students are labeled as social climbing peasants."

"One of the kids at the skateboard park said most of the boarders were upper class, uh, jerks."

She leaned forward and whispered, "That is probably not the word he used."

He shrugged and chuckled. "Same meaning."

"So, what are your classes, Michael Callahan?"

"I'm in the International Baccalaureate program, six courses: history, literature, physics, maths, economics, and Latin." He paused, desperate to keep her talking. "How about you?"

"I'm taking most of those courses. Not Latin, though. I've had enough Latin." She leaned a little closer and stared into his eyes. "Your eyelashes are ridiculous, boyo. Totally wasted on a bloke."

He grinned. "They came with the rest of the package." He batted his eyes a few times for her.

Ciara laughed. "They're grand. Most of my friends would kill to have them."

He chuckled again.

"Am I amusing you, Yank?" she said, an edge in her voice.

"No, no. Sorry. We live in the New Mexico mountains, near Taos Ski Valley, a fabulous resort. My parents took me to ski my first time when I was almost three years old. They slapped goggles on me. My eyelashes pressed against the lens, and it bothered me. So, I asked my mom if she could trim my eyelashes. She freaked." He laughed again. "She tells that story at every opportunity." He paused, then took a chance. "Your eyes are pretty outstanding, too—by the way."

She smiled and opened her mouth to reply—

"Look who's here—the Mexican midget. Got a haircut, huh?"

Michael turned and looked up at the kid who had unceremoniously interrupted his conversation with the intriguing Ciara.

"Who are you?"

The guy was tall, probably near six feet, broad shoulders, sandy-colored hair, and fit. His blue eyes had no welcome in them, and his voice confirmed the bad first impression. Michael had heard that tone before—this was a bully playing to the small knot of boys behind him.

"My big brother was easy on you the other night. He thought you were a girl because of your girly hair."

"Really, dude?" Michael smiled. "Okay, now I get it. He must be one of those tough guys who likes to beat up girls. Didn't work out so well, did it?"

"Listen, you little runt—"

"Séamus Hallums!" Ciara said. "You leave him alone! And tell that brother of yours he better be leaving me alone, too."

"Tell him yerself, girl. I don't know what he sees in you anyway." Hallums stalked away, trailed by his crew.

They watched his procession drift across the cafeteria. Ciara said, "Welcome to St. Georges, Michael." They both laughed. "But be careful around that bloke. He's not as nasty as his big brother, but he's still mean."

CHAPTER FIFTEEN

First Day of Classes
St. George's College

First period was maths. Michael could see that he was going to ace this class. Basic calculus. A nice review for him plus some independent study.

Second period brought Latin. He followed the noisy crowd of students flowing through the older section of the building. The hallway walls were decorated with black-and-white graduation pictures of dozens and dozens of previous St. George's student classes, back into the late 1800s. A glass exhibition case, jammed with athletic trophies collected over almost two centuries, lined the wall of one entire corridor.

He entered the Latin classroom and stopped in surprise. The room was packed with more students than in his maths class. Back in Taos, Latin was an elective rarely taken. A typical class size was three or four students. Conversation buzz died as all eyes turned to scope him out. He gave a small smile and nodded to the group as he made his way to his preferred location in the back of the room.

As he settled behind his desk, the teacher, Ms. Scher, a middle-aged woman with short dark hair speckled with gray, wearing a dark conservative suit and wire-rim glasses, strode in. She moved like Ciara, confident, with an easy smile and demeanor. Many of the students waved and smiled back at her. Clearly, both she and Latin were popular.

She paced across the front of the room to address the class. "Good morning and welcome back. We're going to try a new technique this term by combining Latin I with Latin II." She glanced around the room. "We have some new students to introduce." She looked straight at Michael. "If I'm not mistaken, you are Michael Anthony Callahan?"

"Yes, ma'am."

"And I understand that you are *not* a Mexican. Rather that you are from *New* Mexico. Is that correct?"

"*Si, señora.*"

She laughed. Michael liked her laugh and her friendly attitude.

After speaking a few words of welcome, Ms. Scher opened her laptop computer and said, "We're going to start the year by listening to one of my favorite pieces of music, *O Fortuna* from *Carmina Burana*."

No way! I love that! The idea that a Latin teacher would play cool music in class had never occurred to him. This was one outrageous teacher. Life at St. George's was getting better all the time!

"*Carmina Burana* is Latin for *Songs from Beuern*, the name given to a manuscript of hundreds of poems, mostly from the 11th, 12th, or 13th centuries. The pieces are mostly bawdy, satirical, and critical of society. Especially the Catholic Church. They were written principally in medieval Latin, many by students."

Excited murmurs bubbled up from the class. She had their attention now.

Imagine writing bawdy poems in Latin. And for publication! Maybe in this class? No telling with this teacher.

She leaned over and clicked her computer. Immediately, Michael heard the familiar strains of the first song.

A little over five minutes later, she asked, "How many of you have heard this before?" Everyone raised their hand. She nodded. "I'm not surprised. According to Wikipedia, it's probably the most frequently performed choral work of the 21st century. These poems are seven, eight, or nine hundred years old! Written in Latin, the *lingua franca* of the educated classes of the time. *Carmina Burana* is everywhere these days. In the movies—it's in all sorts of movie trailers, and variations are embedded in almost all action movies, whether you notice it or not."

She paused and swept her gaze around the room. "I want to say that again. Almost all action movies! And on the telly—you'll hear it in the American programs that so many of you watch—*Southpark, The Simpsons, How I Met Your Mother, The Flash*, in adverts like Old Spice. It's played by punk bands, gothic bands, The Trans-Siberian Orchestra, and symphony orchestras across the globe. It is everywhere."

She faced the students. "Ladies and gentlemen, not only the music. The words. Latin is everywhere in your world, realize it or not. It both elevates and is more abstract than English or Irish." She paused. "I am going to raise your linguistic awareness to heights your friends cannot even imagine."

Oh man, oh man, this class is going to be epic!

CHAPTER SIXTEEN

St. George's Dining Room

At lunch, Michael wandered into the enormous dining room. *Smells like boiled cabbage. What a surprise.* His eyes searched the crowd for a friendly face and found a seat across from Ciara at a table away from the other kids. As they ate, they compared notes on their respective morning classes.

Michael said, "I looked at the school website about Latin. It has a listing for L.A. Scher, B.A. (Hons), M.A. Do you know what the L.A. stands for?"

Ciara shook her head. "Nobody knows. It's like a pseudonym."

He chuckled. "That fits. She's not like any teacher I've ever had."

"She's going to work your butt off. I had so much Latin homework it took hours. Great class, though."

"She looks nice. She is, in a different sort of way, very proper and professional. It's awesome."

Ciara sat back in her chair and stared at Michael, as if appraising him. Then, she leaned forward and whispered, "Can I trust you with a secret? Are you trustworthy?"

He made a zipping sound and passed his pinched fingers across his mouth. "I am the Sphinx."

"I went to a death metal concert last term on the other side of Dublin. There she was. She had spiky hair, sparkly makeup, purple wife-beater shirt, purple shorts, purple socks, and purple shoes. Michael, she is not your average St. George's teacher."

"I don't think she's an average anything. She's totally cool." He thought a moment. "*Carmina Burana* is like medieval heavy metal. Now I know she likes death metal, which I don't have on my phone. Maybe I'll do a search and see if I can find some, take it to class. Yeah, death metal in Latin class. She'll love it." He smiled. "It seems appropriate somehow. You know, death metal, dead language." They laughed.

"If you like Ms. Scher so much, Ciara, why aren't you taking Latin anymore?"

"I had my turn with Latin. Seven years, boyo." She finished her meat dish and attacked her salad. "My personal hero is Gráinne Ni Mháille, sometimes pronounced Gráinne O'Malley. You might have heard of her as Granny O'Malley?"

"Nope, nope, and nope."

"She was an Irish queen, some say pirate. She was a bold woman, ahead of her time. She sailed all the way to London in 1593 to negotiate with Queen Elizabeth the First for her son's release from the clutches of the English army. Queen to queen."

"You brought this up because?"

"Neither could speak the other's language, so they spoke Latin."

"Okay, got it." He paused. "She must have been one of your ancestors."

"Why do you say that?" Ciara challenged.

"I can see you going all gangster, fighting challengers to your throne, having the guts to sail to London to have a face-to-face with one of the fiercest and strongest women in history."

Ciara positively preened. "Really, you think that, boyo?"

"Oh yeah. Not a stretch."

She gulped down her tea, a smile on her face. "The reason I don't want to take any more Latin is that I want to take Spanish."

"Really?" asked Michael, surprised. "Why?"

"Because I have never been anywhere. Have you ever read Hemingway's version of Spain, *A Death in the Afternoon*?"

"Sure. And *The Sun Also Rises*."

"Yes. Both. Wonderful books." She eyed him. "And in Spanish, too, I bet."

He nodded.

"Those books helped me fall in love with Spain." She hooked an errant strand of hair behind her ear, a movement he thought exquisitely cool. "But I also have a practical reason. When I graduate, before I go to university, I want to go to Spain and work for a year, just to get out of Ireland. Spanish is my ticket out of here. Because of my Latin background, I aced Spanish I. Skipped Spanish II and am in the advanced Spanish III class. Which is, by the way, really hard."

Opportunity knocked. Michael jumped on it. "I can help with your Spanish homework."

"Really?" She leaned back in her chair, taken by surprise. "You would do that?"

He nodded. "No problem."

"And what do you want from me in return?"

There was an awkward pause as the double meaning of that question hung in the air.

Do not look at her boobs! Do not look at her boobs! Michael felt his face go hot. *She knows what you're thinking, you cretin!*

Her face flashed crimson. "Let me re-phrase that—"

"I know what you mean," he said, relieved. "How about you show me around Dublin, maybe even a trip or two outside the city? You know, a little of the real Ireland?"

"Deal." They shook hands and laughed.

"When do you have history?" he asked.

"Last period."

"Me, too."

She doesn't sound happy. She doesn't want to be in a class with me?

"Is there a problem, Ciara?"

"The problem is the teacher. Our other history teacher retired, so there is no avoiding Mr. Donal Gillmore, M.A., late of Trinity College Dublin."

He relaxed. *At least it's not me.*

"Have you ever heard the phrase 'Never in doubt, frequently in error?'"

"No."

"Well, it applies to Mr. Gillmore." She sniffed. "He's pretentious. Not nice. And he's a bit pink as well. Commonly referred to as 'The Commissar.'"

"Pink?"

"A little too fond of our communist neighbors."

"Really?"

"You'll see."

CHAPTER SEVENTEEN

St. George's

Michael hurried down the corridor to history class, hoping to get a chance to chat a bit with Ciara, but got lost and ended up arriving just in time. The classroom felt like a tomb compared to the cheerful atmosphere in Latin class. Not nearly as many students, a surprise for a required class.

He caught sight of Ciara. Even in a sea of gray-uniformed students where red heads stood out like icebergs, Michael could spot her strawberry-blonde mane. She flashed him a smile that lit up the room and made being there worthwhile. All the desks clustered around her were full of male students. No accident there.

He walked past her desk and smiled. "Hey, Ciara."

She smiled back. "Michael."

The boys around her shot him dirty looks as he headed to his usual nest in the back of the room.

He passed by Mr. Gillmore's bookshelf and slowed to read the titles. *Das Kapital, Marx-Engels Reader, Why Not Socialism?, The Russian Anarchists,* books by Lenin, Guevara, Chomsky, and others. *Holy Cow! Ciara was right! This book collection looks like a library shelf labeled*

"The Best Anarchist, Communist, and Socialist Books of the Past One Hundred Fifty Years." *Pink, she said? This guy's way past pink.*

Mr. Gillmore shuffled into the room. A big man, he had an awkward gait and leaned heavily on his cane. Sporting a three-day growth of gray-speckled beard and dressed in what appeared to be an expensive suit, he still seemed grubby to Michael's eyes, like an ex-athlete going to fat. He also looked grumpy as he slumped into his desk chair.

He gazed around the classroom with a scowl on his face. "Another year, another bloody euro." He spotted Michael. "You must be the faux-Mexican so many people are talking about. I understand that you're American."

"Yes, sir."

"I must tell you up front, Callahan, in the interest of intellectual honesty, that I don't think much of America, or Americans for that matter."

Michael remained silent.

"What, no comeback, no brash outburst about American exceptionalism?"

"I know you don't like America, Mr. Gillmore. I saw your bookshelf."

"I'm surprised you recognized any of those books."

Michael chose to remain silent. *Ciara was right about this guy, wasn't she now?* He smiled at hearing her lilting speech in his imagination.

"Do I amuse you, Callahan?"

"Sorry, Mr. Gillmore. I was thinking of something else."

"See that you pay better attention, or you won't last long in this class."

Mr. Gillmore gave a rambling overview of the course. "At the end of term, we will be examining Napoleon's defeat at Waterloo. Out of curiosity, how many of you have heard of the Battle of Waterloo?"

Everyone raised their hand.

"Anyone have a relative at Waterloo that you can document?"

Three boys raised their hand. Michael slowly raised his own.

"I'm surprised that an American would even know about the battle." All heads turned to look at Michael. A few of them had smirks on their faces.

He said nothing.

Gillmore went on. "Much less claim to have a relative there. Can you prove it?"

"Lieutenant, later Captain, Sean Patrick Callahan."

"Really, Callahan? What unit?" Gillmore challenged.

"He was with the 27th Inniskilling Regiment."

He leaned forward over his desk. "Enlighten us about this particular regiment."

"The 27th Inniskilling was a distinguished unit formed in 1689 and was the only all-Irish regiment present at Waterloo, Mr. Gillmore."

"Very surprising answer, young man." Gillmore laughed. "How did you come to know that?"

"My family has pretty good records of the family tree and most of its branches back more than three hundred years. Prior to Waterloo, my antecedent fought in the Peninsular campaign with the Duke of Wellington."

Gillmore seemed to be enjoying himself. He clasped his hands and laughed. "Tell me about the famous 27th at Waterloo, Callahan."

"The 27th was assembled in a fighting square at the center of Wellington's line and took enormous casualties, almost two-thirds killed or wounded."

"And amongst these big, strong, determined men was a Callahan?"

"The men were certainly strong and determined but more my size than yours, Mr. Gillmore. Average height back then was five-foot-five inches."

"But not your complexion."

A hush fell over the classroom.

Michael felt the heat of a flush creep across his cheeks. *This guy plays hardball.* He remembered to smile. "Probably not."

Michael was the last student out of the classroom.

Ciara was waiting around the first corner, nostrils flared in full fury. "Intellectual honesty, my left foot. The man's a wanker!" Her face flushed bright pink. "Sorry, I don't normally talk like that. But why would he say something so nasty and uncalled for?"

"According to my favorite Irish lass, simply because he's a wanker."

"He's a bloody-minded … oh never mind. He's just bloody-minded, if you ask me." She moved closer and looked Michael in the eyes. "You didn't take offense?"

"I understand that people like him don't like America, Ciara. I've actually been to a communist rally and listened to them rant."

"No, never!"

"There are still lots of commies around Milan. Last summer, I went with my dyedushka. He wanted me to translate."

"Wait! What? In Milan? You speak Italian, too?"

"Relax, Ciara. My grandmother has a family home in Siena. We go there often. We speak Italian in her house. It's not a big deal."

"Not a big deal? Are you mad?" She studied his face. "You just keep the surprises rolling in, don't you now?"

They started walking down the hall toward the Commons. "Gillmore is a communist masquerading as a progressive. I don't like commies," he said. "He doesn't like Americans. Lines are drawn. The difference is that I know more about commies than he knows about me. My advantage."

He changed the subject. "When does your bus leave?"

She checked the hall clock. "About thirty minutes. Why?"

"Why don't we find a quiet spot and do your Spanish homework? We can probably knock it out before then."

She smiled her fabulous smile. *"¿Por qué no? chico?"*

CHAPTER EIGHTEEN

St George's
One Week Later

After classes and another thirty awesome minutes of Spanish homework with Ciara, Michael carried his athletic gear to the gym, changed into running clothes in the locker room, stuffed his backpack into an unlockable locker, and headed out to the athletic fields.

There were dozens of students scattered all over the extensive fields, either in intramural or inter-scholastic teams. He scoped out the soccer pitch where he would prefer to be working out and caught a glimpse of Séamus Hallums running drills with his teammates.

The track was first-rate with a spongy artificial surface. It looked like a standard eight-lane four-hundred-meter track, superbly maintained like everything at St. George's College. He found a plot of grass alongside the track and started his stretches, then some yoga. He focused on working the major muscle groups because he was stiff and slow, having been uncharacteristically idle during the past three months while his leg healed. He needed to get in shape for the winter snowboard competitions. The little skateboarding he had done had shown him that he had a long way to go.

He started his run slowly, paying attention to his mended leg. No pain. Yet. He gradually picked up the pace. Still good. He tried some side-to-side movements, like cutting and quick starts. They hurt. *Just run straight ahead, boyo. Take it easy!*

He reined himself in and finished four laps without any more pain. Feeling frisky, he did some handstands, then walked on his hands in the grassy infield. Threw in some forward rolls to celebrate the simple joy of moving his body without pain. Emboldened, he did a flip. Then another. No pain. He smiled. *Excellent!*

Michael flopped down in the grass and rolled over on his back. Puffy clouds filled the sky, and he could actually see big patches of blue. It hadn't rained in over forty-eight hours, probably an Irish record. He laughed out loud and wriggled like a dog in the thick, lush grass, a by-product of all that Irish rain. It had been a long time since he had felt so good. *A few weeks of this, then maybe some parkour moves, and life will be sweet. So sweet!*

Startled by an air horn blast, he looked around to see most of the teams ending their workout. *Must be the signal to get the non-boarding athletes out in time to catch the busses home.*

He settled back to watch the teams trooping toward the gym locker rooms.

"Hey, Runt." Séamus Hallums flipped him off the Irish way, with two fingers, as he trotted past.

Nice. *Wonder why he's like he is!*

Michael laughed and started his trek toward the gymnasium, almost last in a long line of sweaty athletes. The locker room was crowded and stunk like—well—a boys locker room. He grabbed his clothes and his backpack and headed back toward his dorm for a shower and dinner. *After dinner, I'll hit the books. I think tonight it's going to be Latin.*

The next morning, Michael made his way through the dining room food line. He paused to search the room for Ciara, off by herself at a table in the far corner, face buried in a textbook. As he approached, she looked up and smiled her fabulous smile, then motioned for him to sit. He slid in next to her.

"How are you today, Ciara?"

Another smile. "I'm in great form, boyo."

He caught a whiff of her scent. She smelled wholesome. No, not quite the right word. Maybe unique was better. Something distinctive, something he couldn't define—sort of like the smell of the sagebrush that stretched across the mesa around Taos, which was ridiculous because there was no sagebrush within three thousand miles of Ireland in any direction. Still, he knew he would never forget what she smelled like. *Unique.* Good name for a perfume. *Wholesome*, not so much.

He eyed his grease-fried breakfast. *This is going to take some getting used to.*

"*Señor Bolivia*, see any llamas today, *amigo?*" Michael looked up to see Séamus Hallums towering over him with his trademark smirk on his face.

"What?"

"Doesn't *amigo* mean friend in Spanish?" asked Séamus with a laugh.

"Not the way you say it."

Behind Séamus, as always, stood his three followers. Michael had begun to think of them as three remoras following a shark. Hallums muttered something to his drones, and they all laughed at some private joke, then wandered away.

Ciara swiveled to look at Michael. "Why did he call you *Señor Bolivia*? Shouldn't he say *Señor Boliviano*? Isn't that more correct?" She looked puzzled. "And why *Señor Bolivia* in the first place?"

Michael shook his head. *I haven't told anybody I was born in Bolivia.* Then, he knew. *Oh no!* He grabbed for his backpack, dug through it. Books and papers. School stuff.

He looked at Ciara. "My passport's gone!"

A student aide from the school's administrative offices approached and beckoned to Michael. "Callahan, the headmaster wants to speak with you. Now."

Now what? Am I going to be deported?

"Michael, is this serious?"

He shrugged, determined not to show how scared he was. "Maybe."

She leaned against him, pressing her shoulder into his. "I'm going with you." She stopped and pulled back. "Sorry. May I come with you?"

He nodded, still a bit overwhelmed.

They entered the Administration office and were waved into the headmaster's office. "Good morning, Miss Harrington. Callahan." He looked back to Ciara. "Please wait outside, Miss Harrington. I need to speak to Michael alone."

He shut the door, then pointed to a plastic bowl on his desk. "The cleaners turned this in this morning." In the bowl was a soggy mass of paper. Michael recognized the torn blue cover. His passport.

Michael sighed. *Is anything ever going to go right here?*

"They found it stopping up a toilet in the locker room. I have a copy of your visa in your file, but you'll have to get another passport, young man. Soon."

"Yes, Headmaster," Michael said in a soft voice. He felt numb.

"Any idea who would do such a thing, Callahan?"

Michael just stared. *I know exactly who it was.* He shook his head.

The headmaster nodded. "I thought you'd say that."

Is he smiling? He knows I'm covering for somebody. And he probably knows who it is.

"Is that all, sir? I'll go to the embassy this week. Promise."

The headmaster handed Michael the bowl. "You'll need this." He paused.

"Why don't you bring me your new passport? I'll keep it in the school safe."

Michael related the incident to Ciara as they walked back toward the cafeteria.

"Séamus?" she asked.

"Who else?"

"He's an *eejit*. Thick as two planks, he is. And what are you going to do about it, boyo?"

He thought for a moment. It was nice having a friend alongside. Especially Ciara. "Do you believe in karma?"

"No. Do you?"

"Yes is the short answer."

"Not a very Catholic answer, *Señor Bolivia.*"

He shrugged. "It's a standard Taos answer. Lots of unconventional philosophical concepts float around Taos. One common expression is 'you reap what you sow.' But back to the real issue here. I know he did it. We know he did it. He knows we know. That's what he gets off on—thinking we can't do anything. What he doesn't know is the headmaster has this figured out and he'll be watching Séamus pretty closely. One day, the world will come crashing down on our good friend, Séamus, courtesy of St. George's College, something far worse than you and I can dish out. The headmaster has a bigger club than we do. That's karma."

Ciara said, "The headmaster expelled Séamus' big brother last term, the bloke you punched out in the pub. That's why the méara and the Superintendent have it in for him and the school."

"Now I get it. No real surprise there."

"I am so sorry about your passport. I just know Séamus is up to something dodgy."

"We'll deal with it."

CHAPTER NINETEEN

St. George's College
Dormitories

Michael opened his laptop, entered a few commands, and after a few seconds, Fabian's familiar dusky face appeared, topped, as always, with his beat-up straw cowboy hat.

"Hey, Dude," Michael said. "*Hola* from across the big blue."

"What are you doing, man? You're not supposed to call back to the States for another month."

Michael shrugged. "Just wanted to hear the sound of an unaccented voice."

"The Irish giving you a hard time, bro? Are you homesick?"

Michael hesitated. "Not sure."

"You've traveled more than anybody I know. I thought you'd be hardcore."

"Yeah, but this is different. People here don't seem to like me very much."

"Give it time, dude. You've been there, what, three weeks?"

"Yeah, easy to say. But right now, it totally sucks."

"And you, by the way, seem to have picked up a bit of the Irish brogue, amigo."

"Can't be helped. I'm surrounded by Irish people all day, every day."

"Yeah, I remember when you came back from Australia last year. I had to make you speak Tiwa until you lost that Aussie accent and I could understand you again."

Michael smiled despite himself. "Ha! We linguists are like that, you know. Pick up accents like you pick up fleas."

"Yeah, yeah. You've told me that, amigo. But I wouldn't have believed it if your babushka hadn't said it, too."

Michael chuckled. "Nobody messes with her."

"No kidding."

"The St. George's computer classroom is awesome. You would be in heaven, evil computer genius that you are." He laughed. "And I bet there are kids here would put you to shame."

"Never happen, dude, never happen. Any hackers?"

"Not that anybody here would tell me."

"Hey man, get out there and make some friends. Get a girlfriend even."

Michael drummed his fingers on the desktop. "Actually, I do have one friend. I'm helping with her Spanish. She's going to take me on a tour of Dublin."

"Oh ho, a female? Is she a human female? An actual Irish human female? Lemme guess, red hair, nice legs, great figure."

"It's not like that, Fabian."

"If she's right, she's the only friend you'll need. What's she look like?"

"Good-bye, Fabian. I have to write a paper for history class."

"Oh man, you can't sign off like that, leave me hangin'. More, I want more."

"Adios, amigo. You told me I wasn't supposed to call back home, and you're right."

CHAPTER TWENTY

DOWNTOWN DUBLIN

It started out as yet another gray day to tour Dublin, but Michael was excited to meet Ciara at her bus stop. She was rocking jeans, a green sweater, a blue scarf that exactly matched her gorgeous eyes, and a dark blue raincoat, which he now knew as a *mac* in Ireland. They rode together into the town center.

Downtown was a labyrinth, cobblestone side streets and impressive modern avenues, old stone buildings alongside modern glass-walled offices. Dubliners were out in force on the crowded sidewalks despite the overcast skies.

As they passed Dublin Castle, Michael remembered Nate's words. "Ciara, do you know there's a tunnel under the castle?"

She rolled her eyes. "I'm from Dublin, ya git. Everybody knows that."

"Oh." *Nice, Michael. Very smooth.*

The bus crossed the River Liffey over the Grafton Bridge and stopped at the top of Grafton Street where they got off. This was a crowded pedestrian thoroughfare, a massive shopping area pulsing with energy, and a favorite stop for tourists and locals. Colorful buildings lined the wide boulevard, which hosted high-end shops, restaurants, and pubs. Merchandise spilled out of many shops onto the sidewalks. Street entertainers dotted the mall, playing music on guitars, Irish harps, saxophones, and even a couple of screeching bagpipes. Ciara seemed fascinated by the singing and stopped for a listen at almost every group.

"Many of these musicians are poor like me. Too proud to beg, so they play music to live."

She dug into her pockets for some change for each group until she ran out of money. Only then did she allow Michael to pay for anything.

Ciara led him past the statue of the famous fictitious Dublin fishmonger, Molly Malone, and through the gates to Trinity College, Dublin (TCD). Facing the main college square, she said, "This is where I wanted to bring you today. This is my personal goal, the reason I work so hard at St. George's."

They started down into the college grounds. "TCD was founded in 1592 by Queen Elizabeth I. It's one of the oldest universities in the English-speaking world, one of the so-called seven ancient universities." She stopped and stared at the imposing Georgian gray stone buildings. Her eyes never stopped moving and she had a smile on her face. Michael could feel her excitement, her love of the school. Finally, she sighed. "It's the best school in Ireland and is me chance to move up in the world. I'm not ashamed of my roots but I want to help me ma, get her a better house, some nicer things. She had me too young, dropped out of the workforce to take care of me and me da in his sickness." She turned to look at Michael. "She sacrificed her life for me. Now she works two jobs to keep us fed."

"Tough lady."

"That she is," Ciara said, fierce pride in her voice. "She inspired me to fight for the scholarship to St. George's. Without it, I wouldn't have a chance."

They walked past more immense buildings and swaths of green grassy areas to the main college square. Ciara kept up a running commentary, like she was a tour guide.

"Here's the Library of Trinity College, the largest in Ireland," she said, pointing to a huge, stately stone building. "It is our version of your Library of Congress. Massive." She slid her arm through his. "Come on, I want to show you something I love, something magic."

When she touched him, Michael totally lost his focus on the college. His mind exploded, and he nearly fell down. *Get real, Michael. Ciara isn't interested in romance. She just wants to show you the school, and she wants to keep you from falling down a manhole or something before she can get you there.* Still, he wondered. And hoped.

Inside, the library was cavernous. Huge dark oak shelves stuffed with books filled room after room. They made their way through the milling crowds of visitors. Excited, Ciara pulled him along. They entered The Long Room, which was massive as she had promised. Stunning high ceilings and multiple floors lined with shelves loaded with books created a majestic atmosphere.

"Here we have *The Book of Kells*," she whispered, eyes shining. "The Four Gospels, handwritten and illustrated by monks around about the year 800 Anno Domini." She spoke reverently as she pointed to a glass display case containing two book chapters, one ornately colored and decorated, the other open to two pages of the Latin text. "It's the world's most famous medieval manuscript. All written and illustrated by hand. And it's gorgeous!"

She's impressed. Impressed and proud of this wonderful book. Proud as any Irish person could be over her country's treasures, just like the rush I had in Washington D.C., looking at the Declaration of Independence and the Constitution. How cool is that!

He was overwhelmed by her enthusiasm, zest for life, determination to meet all challenges and wrestle them into submission. Nothing was going to stop this girl. She was a force of nature. He was determined not to touch her even though his hands kept reaching for her, itching to touch her. He wondered if her skin felt as soft as it looked.

They left the college grounds and Ciara led him toward St. Stephen's Green to catch a bus. Michael insisted on buying her an ice cream and they sat on a park bench to eat it.

"Why are you smiling at me like that?" she asked.

"Sorry." He felt his face grow hot in embarrassment. "Didn't realize I was staring."

"Well?" she demanded.

"Well what?"

"Why were you staring?"

"You remind me of my *babushka*. Sorry, my grandmother."

"The artist?"

He nodded.

She thought for a moment. "You love your grandmother?"

"Oh yeah, big time. She's amazing. Nobody says no to my grandmother and gets away with it. Nobody. Not my father, not my mother, not my grandfather. Even the mayor of Taos got steamrollered by my babushka a couple times." He laughed. "I told her once that she should run for Congress. Then maybe Washington would start doing its job, start getting things done. She said nobody could get those people to work together."

A slow, gentle rain began falling as they walked in silence to the bus stop.

"There's tons more to see in Dublin, Michael. But I have to go to work."

"Maybe another time?" he asked, hoping.

"Sure." She smiled. "It's been a grand afternoon. *Muchas gracias por el helado, chico.*" She flashed another one of her fabulous smiles as she boarded her bus. He watched it pull away.

What a girl.

He leaned against the pole that held up the bus schedule. His thoughts drifted to Ciara. In his mind, he heard her laugh. Her energy level was extraordinary—restless, uncontained. It matched his own. He felt more comfortable moving than holding still. So was she.

Strong women were the norm in his family—mother, grandmother, aunts, cousins. Only a strong woman would be right for him, no question. He smiled to himself. And Ciara was a kick-ass girl for sure.

Undeniably cool.

He had to face facts. He was crushing on Ciara, big time. And all of this came to him while standing in the rain, waiting for a bus. Weird.

CHAPTER TWENTY-ONE

St. George's College
History Class

Mr. Gillmore was late. Students kicked back and relaxed, whispering hopes that he wouldn't show up. Michael watched from his desk in the last row as the boys seated around Ciara tried to chat her up. Maybe he imagined it, but she didn't seem very interested.

The hopes of a teacher-less class were dashed as Gillmore limped in fifteen minutes late, leaning heavily on his cane. He threw his briefcase on his desk and snarled something about his knee. He sank carefully into his leather chair, then leaned forward and removed a sheaf of papers from the case.

"The assignment was an analysis of the Battle of Hastings. Four pages. That should have been quite clear." He gestured to the boy in the front row to take the papers and hand them out. Gillmore kept one.

Murmurs from the students indicated surprise and dismay. Michael could see some of the papers scattered about the room, covered with red slashes. Gillmore must have had a rough night with his knee when he graded the reports. Or was simply being a jerk.

Gillmore looked at Michael and held up his paper. It was marked with an enormous X across the first page. "I said for you to write a composition, Callahan. Not plagiarize it. This must be straight out of some online college term paper factory."

Surprised, Michael blurted, "Not true, Mr. Gillmore. I wrote it, footnotes and all."

"I don't believe it, Callahan."

"My grandfather is a graduate of the United States Military Academy at West Point, our version of Britain's Sandhurst. He knows everything about every important battle in history, from the Greeks to the present."

"Ha! So, he wrote this!"

"No. He taught me about Hastings, among other battles. It was sort of a game we played, toy soldiers, sand tables, the whole bit since I was a kid."

"We don't use the word kid in Ireland to describe children, Callahan. Here a 'kid' is a baby goat."

Michael sighed. *What a bozo.* "Fine. But I have been studying military history with my grandfather, a major general, since I was a child."

Gillmore shifted in his chair and grimaced in pain as he moved his leg. "You are still a child, Callahan."

He's goading you, Michael me boy. Calm down. "In the big scheme of things, Mr. Gillmore, you are correct. I am a post-pubescent child, an adolescent child, a young adult. Your choice. But I did write that paper, whatever you try to label me."

The two locked eyes.

"Pick a battle, any major battle of the Middle Ages, Mr. Gillmore. Maybe the Hundred Years' War. I can give you a detailed synopsis of each and every one, right now. Crécy. Poitiers. Agincourt. Castillon." Michael glared at his teacher. "Go ahead, pick one."

Gillmore slapped his desk, then pointed to the door. "Get out of my class!"

What?

"You're throwing me out?" Michael glanced at Ciara, who appeared to be in shock, then shifted back to the red-faced teacher.

"Do not return. Report to the headmaster."

You have got to be kidding me!

"Now, Callahan. You don't belong here."

Wow, that didn't take long! Michael sat for a moment, sorting through his emotions. Then, he smiled and nodded. *This is the first time in my life where I've enjoyed being told that I don't belong.* He stood and grabbed his backpack.

Michael stared at his teacher as he strode up to the front of the room, bent over the desk, and snatched his paper. "I'll take this, if you don't mind."

"Get back here with that!"

"I'll give this to the headmaster and let him evaluate it."

Michael spent the next thirty minutes seething in a chair in the Administrative section while waiting for the headmaster to return from a meeting off campus.

He stood as the headmaster swept into his office and motioned for Michael to take a seat inside.

"I've just had an interesting chat on the phone with Mr. Gillmore, Callahan."

"Yes sir. I expected that."

"Why don't you tell me your side of the issue?"

Michael recited his rehearsed speech then handed over the paper. "This is it, sir."

The headmaster settled back into his chair and studied the pages. He looked up. "You wrote this?"

Oh, not that again! "Yes, sir. Every word. Original."

The headmaster put the paper down and thought for several long moments. "Ms. Scher is delighted with your progress in Latin. And I understand your maths teacher has you tutoring some of your fellow students."

Really? How does he even know that?

"Don't look so surprised, lad. I am the headmaster. You are one of my students. It's my job to know how my students are doing. By all accounts, you are an outstanding student."

"Not according to my history teacher," Michael muttered. "Sorry, my former history teacher."

"No. It doesn't appear so, does it now?" The headmaster settled back into his leather chair again and steepled his fingers, lost in thought. "Do you enjoy history, Michael?"

"Of course, sir. History has, like, everything. Civilizations being built, then torn down. Wars, greed, hate, love, sex, art, power grabs. Huge disruptions. Magnificent creations. Heroes and villains galore."

"And you asked Mr. Gillmore to pick a battle, any battle, and you would give him a verbal summary?"

Michael nodded. "Specifically, battles of the Hundred Years' War. Yes."

"And he chose to ignore your challenge?"

"Told me I didn't belong in his class."

The headmaster said, "Tell me about Crécy."

Michael paused for a moment to organize his thoughts. "August 1346. Crécy was probably the bloodiest, most lopsided battle of the war, and a massive defeat for the French. It featured English defensive tactics using archers and dismounted knights against French aggressive offensive tactics favoring mounted heavy cavalry." He spoke for almost ten minutes, pointing, waving his hands around, describing the battle as if it happened yesterday. The headmaster interrupted to ask a few questions about specific points, which showed he was no slouch in the history department.

"You know, Michael, before I took this position, I taught history at Trinity College Dublin." He paused. "You need a history credit this term. Why don't we do this—every week, I'll give you a subject or a book. Then you return and give me a summary, say for twenty minutes. I will quiz you and grade you on your grasp of the subject, the organization of your report, and your vocabulary."

"Really?"

The headmaster smiled. "That's the way we do it at Oxford and Cambridge."

Oh yeah! This is going to be fun. Michael breathed a sigh of relief. *I am now smelling like a rose.* "Deal, Headmaster. Thank you, sir."

"Welcome to St. George's College, young man."

CHAPTER TWENTY-TWO

St. George's Commons Room
Monday morning Study Hall

The St. George's Commons Room was enormous, Hogwarts big. High ceiling, rimmed with windows that provided light, lots of oak along the walls, extensive bookshelves, and long oak tables. Students were scattered randomly, most with books open, papers piled beside them. Individual desks lined three walls, complete with personal computers. Students already occupied all the desks.

Michael made a point of visiting the room at least twice a day to see if he could accidently bump into Ciara. He spotted her at her own table and made a beeline toward her.

"Missed you at breakfast today," he said. She gave him a preoccupied smile. She was surrounded by books scattered about. Typical. Studying was always on her mind. When she studied, she totally immersed herself. Bombs could go off in the room and she wouldn't even notice.

He sat next to her. *Man, she even smells beautiful.* She toyed with her hair whenever she read a book. He loved it. "I went fishing this weekend."

"Mmmm," she said, head down, her eyes flicked back to her maths book.

"One of the guys, sorry, the father of one of the lads at the skateboard park has a fishing lease on the river near Luddington. Gave me permission to fish."

He paused. No reaction. "It was a great day."

Her eyes stayed locked on her book.

"What did you do, Ciara?"

After a long moment, she said, "I worked a double shift on Saturday and the lunch shift Sunday. And studied."

Oops.

He tried again. "You like to fish?"

She didn't even look up. "Never been." She turned a page. "Are you ready for the maths test tomorrow?"

"Yes." Actually, he hadn't even thought about it. *Piece of cake.*

"I'm not. I have two big tests this week. And two shifts at the pub. I'll be all weekend working for them. Not to mention an oral interview in Spanish next week and another history paper."

He wanted to say they could speak Spanish on the way out to the fishing area and back, but clearly fly-fishing was not high on her list of priorities. What bothered him most was with her increasing academic load, she didn't seem too keen on spending time with him outside school anymore. He was down with any activity that would give him an excuse to be with her. Dominoes, mah jhong, ballet, whatever.

Another boy sauntered over. Michael looked up to see the rugby team captain, Galen McPherson, a superb athlete and class president. Big, impressive, and handsome with reddish-blond hair and striking physique, the male model on the St. George's College brochure, and a shoo-in for Trinity College. Pretty much everything Michael was not. *Dude probably has to shave twice a day.* Michael, like many Native Americans, had smooth skin and probably wouldn't be able to grow a beard until he was forty.

The big boy sat, gave Michael a sideways glance, then faced Ciara.

"Top of the mornin' to ye, Ciara, me luv."

Ciara looked up and gave him a half smile. "Hello, Galen."

"The rugby team is hosting a party Saturday night. I'd like you to go with me. How about it?"

"Thank you, Galen, but I'll have to say no once again. I'm terrible busy." She pointed to her books. "I'm way behind, and the term's not half done."

McPherson's eyes narrowed. Then, he smiled and said, "Perhaps another time then."

Ciara watched him walk away. "Why can't they take no for an answer?"

"Who?"

"Boys. That bloke has asked me out three times this term. Why can't they pay attention? They keep asking me out. I keep saying no." She slammed her maths book shut. "I don't have time for a boyfriend. Never had one. Never will. I need to work. I need to study so I can go to Trinity College and make something of meself. All they want is to stick their tongue down your throat. Disgusting. Or worse, get you into trouble. Not me. Not ever!"

She took another look at Galen's retreating form.

"Totally lost me concentration." She looked at Michael and chuckled. "He is a handsome bloke, though, is he not?"

"Sure makes me feel like a shrimp."

She laughed. "I think people tend to underestimate you, Michael, partly because of your size. And you're easy going, funny, and cute."

"Thanks a lot."

"No, no, I mean that your exterior—as lovely as it is—disguises the real Michael Callahan. You are brilliant in school, a wonderful athlete, very clever with languages, and have a heart that is, figuratively speaking, as big as a house. And capable without arrogance." She leaned into his space and smiled. "Unlike most blokes, I might add." She started to gather her papers.

Then, why won't you go out on the town with me anymore? He needed to know the answer.

He opened his mouth to challenge her. Then, it hit him. *Oh no!* He had evolved into the most dreaded of all social positions. He was her *friend!* Almost a *brother!* *Yikes!*

CHAPTER TWENTY-THREE

ST GEORGE'S COLLEGE

Ms. Scher ran her Latin class with a casual benevolence Michael had only witnessed with his grandfather. At the start of every class, the second-year students raced to rearrange the classroom for the day's lesson without being told. Homework was already done and placed on her desk. Students were attentive and worked harder for her than for the average, hard-driving teacher. As Michael had done for years of homeschooling, trying to anticipate his grandfather's wishes and excel in his classwork.

She took attendance with a simple glance around the room. "It seems that the flu has taken its toll here. You remaining second-years cluster over there and brainstorm end-of-term project proposals while I take the lone first-year and work with him in the back of the room."

They settled down in a rear corner. "Well, Michael, it looks like you're on the spot today. You speak Spanish, I understand?"

"Yes, ma'am."

"Any other languages, perhaps Romance languages?"

He hesitated. "I speak Italian as well."

She nodded. "Excellent. That's a good step, Michael, but you have a long way to go. Latin is the root of those languages, but it is not Italian nor is it Spanish."

"That's why I'm here."

After thirty minutes of line-by-line translation of the Bayeux Tapestry and a lively discussion of subject-verb agreement and word function, she said, "I have to say that you are doing very well in this class."

"Thank you. I spend a lot of time on it."

"How do you know so much about inflectional endings?"

He hesitated. Finally, he said. "Maybe because Russian has six cases as well."

"Russian? You speak Russian?"

He nodded. "Please don't tell anybody."

"Why ever not?"

He sighed. *You won't understand.* "I'm already way different here. I don't need any more ways to stand out."

"Why not? Why not celebrate being different? The things that mark you as different or weird as a teenager make you interesting as an adult. I think you're an amazing young man."

"Yeah, well, I'm short and brown, and I'm in Ireland. I don't need kids here to know that I speak four languages. I'd be a freak. It's like being back in my own family."

"You're a freak in your family? That's hard to imagine."

"That's what I think. They're all blonds and tall."

"How old were you when you were adopted?"

"Two months."

"So, they are the only family you've ever known?"

He nodded. "My birth parents died."

"They live on in your DNA, Michael. They are immortalized that way."

"And the Callahans?" he challenged. "I can't immortalize them, not with DNA anyway."

"When you have children, your Callahan parents will imprint them with memories. If your parents are anything like what you've described to me, they will be all over your children, loving them, teaching them. Passing on their Callahan culture to them. Don't shortchange your parents, Michael. I'm sure they love you very much."

Wow, that's a new way of looking at it. This is one amazing teacher.

"What about you, Ms. Scher? How are you connected to your family?"

She studied him for a moment, as if thinking over her answer. "Most of my relatives were loaded into boxcars and sent to gas chambers during the Holocaust. My grandparents were survivors. We had to re-invent our family. And we did it because we had no choice."

Sheesh. Just when I work up a great case of "poor me," somebody comes along with a worse situation. Like the saying, "I cursed my life because I had no shoes until I met a man who had no feet."

"Where did you learn Russian?" she asked. "Family? Friends?"

"It's pretty complicated. My maternal grandmother was raised in Italy by Russian parents who escaped Russia after the revolution. She married my grandfather who was in the United States Air Force. Four kids later, he was shot down in Vietnam. Because of his technical background, the North Vietnamese sent him to the Soviet Union where he spent thirty years as a prisoner. When he was rescued, we all moved to Taos where he homeschooled me in Russian. So, I speak Russian with my grandfather and mostly Italian with my grandmother. Spanish and English with my parents, brothers, and friends."

"You are very lucky. You shouldn't be shy about your abilities. You should be proud. Polyglots are not common in America like they are in Europe." She started to gather up her papers. "I'm about to start a new project for the Latin II students that I'd like you to join."

"Okay. What is it?"

"The Pope sends tweets out weekly in Latin. I want the Latin IIs to translate those tweets, then write responses to the Pope, also in Latin."

"Tweet the Pope? No way!"

She smiled. "Yes, way."

"I'm down for that, Ms. Scher. Thanks!"

"And if I may be so bold, the next time you're on the Internet, look up Monty Python's Latin lesson. It is one of the funniest videos out there. Let's have some fun this term, shall we?"

CHAPTER TWENTY-FOUR

St. George's Dining Room
Monday lunch

Today, the dining room smelled like meat. Probably beef. And potatoes, of course. Since his arrival in Ireland, Michael had eaten more potatoes than he thought possible.

He spied Ciara at a table by herself. She sat, face in her hands, eyes closed.

He slid into a seat across from her.

"Missed you at breakfast this morning," he said.

She stared at him through her fingers, eyes dull. She appeared listless. Exhausted.

"You look tired, my friend."

"Thanks a lot."

"No," he said. "I didn't mean it like that. Something's up with you, and I want to know what it is."

After a moment, she leaned toward him, palms on the table, and hissed, "My mother cleans houses as a second job, all right? She's sick, all right? So I'm helping, all right?"

Ah. Got it. Plus probably two shifts at the pub. "What kind of houses?" he said, keeping his voice neutral.

"House houses," she snapped. "AirBnB houses."

"You have one tonight?"

She slumped back in her seat and said in a tired voice, "Two, actually. I have to go home after classes and fix my brother's dinner and take care of me mum. Then, clean the houses. So, I'll be late again tomorrow."

"I can help. Let me help you."

"You?" She laughed, scorn in her voice. "I bet you've never cleaned a house in your life. People like you have people like me to do the dirty work."

"Ciara, I live on a ranch. We have horses. I muck out the stables. I feed the animals. I help in the fields. I cut and bale hay. I fix stuff. We all do. Cleaning a house would be a snap over some of the things I've had to do."

She stared at him for a long moment. "You would do that for me?"

He nearly said he'd take a bullet for her but decided that would be way over the top. "Sure. *Somos amigos, verdad?*"

She hesitated.

"Okay, I'll throw in a Spanish lesson. Make it a legit class. Storytelling. Vocabulary. Subjunctive."

"Oh no, not the subjunctive!" she said in mock horror and covered her face with her arms. "I knew you had an evil plan, boyo. Torture me, will ya?"

Michael arrived at the first house to be cleaned ten minutes early. Ciara hugged him. That was all the appreciation he needed. He'd do houses every day for that kind of payback.

She started barking orders. "I'll do the kitchen. You strip the beds and hoover the carpets. Bathrooms and toilets. Then, we'll make the beds together. There's three of them."

He gave her a mock salute and headed upstairs.

Later, when they met at the master bedroom and started in on the beds, she said, "I'll have my Spanish lesson now, if you please, *Señor Boliviano.*"

"*Sí, señorita.*" He hesitated. "First, I'd like to tell you a story in English. Okay?"

She nodded.

"Do you know what *acequias* are?"

She thought a moment. "Spanish irrigation systems?"

"*Excelente, chica.* Brought to Spain by the Moors, imported to the New World by the Spanish. Lots of little towns and villages in New Mexico have them, basically communal irrigation systems. The whole town pitches in to keep the ditches clean and functioning."

"Wasn't there a movie about them?"

"*Sí*, based on the novel *The Milagro Bean Field War* by John Nichols, who lives in Taos, by the way. Anyhow, one time at the ranch, I had to go out to the acequia at night to close the mother gate, which controls the flow of water to the fields. No moon, overcast, so there were no stars. It was pitch dark, like you've never seen here in a city. Black. A few ground lights in the distance."

She nodded. "We Irish have a saying, 'blacker than the inside of a cow with its eyes closed and its tail down.'"

Michael laughed. "That's exactly how it was. Anyhow, my flashlight started fading. I had just had a fight with my father who told me to check my equipment but I wouldn't listen. Of course, he was right again. I went out all alone as usual, but this time it was different. Something else was out there. I could feel it. Something big ran through the sage. I dropped my flashlight and ran, crashed into the acequia, and landed in the ditch. Thought I was going to drown in about eighteen inches of freezing water. I thrashed my way out of the ditch, total panic. Fired my pistol until it was empty, then I tripped into the ditch again. Lost the pistol in the water. I was scared fartless."

Ciara laughed so hard she nearly fell down. She flopped on the bed. "Sorry, boyo. But I can totally see that."

"It's funny now but not then. I hid in the barn until I got myself under control, then went home, covered in mud. It's a family joke now, but man, it was scary then. I never told them about what really happened. They think I just fell into the acequia and tease me about that.

"Nobody knows the real story, Ciara. You're the only person I've ever told."

"Not even Fabian?"

"Especially not Fabian."

"But he's your best friend."

"My best friend does know. Now."

Suddenly Ciara smiled, and it was like the sun came out. Totally.

He said, "Let's go knock out the next house. Then, let me take you to dinner."

"Oh, Michael, you've done enough. I'm way ahead of schedule now. I can do the next one alone."

"Please. You take care of everybody else. Let me take you to a pub and buy you dinner. Let the people in the pub serve you for a change, take care of you for an hour or so. You deserve it. Then, I'll take you home so you can get some rest."

She looked at him for a long moment. "Why not? But just an hour. No longer."

"Yes, ma'am."

CHAPTER TWENTY-FIVE

DEVON BUCKLEY'S PUB
DUBLIN

They sat at a small table in the corner of the bustling pub, meal almost finished. Michael looked at Ciara and congratulated himself. As she ate, she perked up, more smiles, more animated, less tension. She was nearly back to her effervescent self.

Ciara set down her fork and looked him in the eyes. "You're different from anyone I've ever known, boyo. More mature for one thing. You are way ahead of the rest of the blokes here."

He felt that familiar stabbing pain in his chest. "I know I'm different. I don't look like my Callahan family, I don't look like anybody here, either. That's my problem." He stared down at his plate of shepherd's pie. "You'll never understand what it's like to be adopted."

"You're right. And since you don't know who your birth parents were, you'll never have an established bloodline that those upper-class aristocrats attach such importance to. It's just breeding, Michael, like racehorses. Not a big deal."

"Yeah," he said. "There's a great movie, *Trading Places*, that has two rich guys betting on culture versus breeding."

"The age-old question, culture or breeding. Environment or genetics."

"That's the question—or one of the questions, all right."

"Have you ever been to Bolivia?" she asked.

He nodded. "On one of our trips to Australia, we took the long way around and went through Bolivia. Stayed a few days. We went to La Paz and Cochabamba where I was born."

"And? How did you feel?"

He shrugged. "The country is beautiful and the people nice. I thought something inside me might scream 'Here I am, back in my own country.'"

"Did it?"

"Sadly, no. No lightning bolt. No nothing. My DNA totally let me down. I didn't fit in there, either. I was a foreigner camouflaged to look Bolivian."

Ciara shifted in her chair, a thoughtful look on her face. "Michael, take a baby born, say in Peru, and place her in a French family. She'll grow up French, won't she? Or a French baby placed in an Australian family or an Indian family will be Australian or Indian."

He said nothing.

"It's even biblical, boyo. Look at Moses, a poor Jewish boy raised in Pharaoh's household like royalty."

Michael laughed. "Never thought of that. But I'm not in his league."

"Of course not. But even he had a crisis of identity. Most people have it. Not all. But I'll wager more than seventy-five per cent of the students in our school are troubled by the question of who they really are. Just like you, Michael.

"Haven't you read any Michener novels, boyo? How Scandinavian girls flock to Spain in search of swarthy Mediterranean men because all the men at home are blond and think like Scandinavians? Act like Scandinavians? The girls are looking for something different."

He shook his head.

"What? There's a famous author you haven't read? Something that I know that you don't know?"

He rolled his eyes, then chuckled. "So, is that the real reason that you want to spend a gap year in Spain? To scope out nearly naked, swarthy men sunning themselves on the beach?"

Ciara laughed. "Perhaps. Maybe a little." She took a sip of her mineral water. "I don't mean you're different because you're American and look different. You think differently than the boys around here. You're different inside."

"And outside."

She leaned forward and slapped the table with her hand. "I don't like you because of your brown skin, O Swarthy One! And I don't like you in spite of your brown skin, either. *Jaysus, boyo.* Sometimes, Michael, you say the dumbest things. What is it you Yanks say? You've got a chip on your shoulder? It's like you're trying to make yourself miserable."

He looked into her eyes and smiled. "I'm not miserable right now, Ciara."

They took the last bus of the night to the stop nearest her house. Michael insisted on walking her the three long blocks to her door.

The neighborhood was dark and smelled like recent rain. The streets glistened in the dim glow cast by the occasional streetlights. The houses were clustered tightly together, not quite rundown, not quite prosperous. They walked down the middle of the street.

Michael took her elbow to steer her away from a pothole. He sucked in a deep breath, then slowly slid his fingers down the inside of her arm. His fingertips traced across her palm, closed gently around hers for a couple heartbeats. Their fingers laced themselves together. She did not pull away.

Holding her hand was sublime. No other word for it. It was the most natural thing in the world. He wondered why he had waited so long.

A silence descended between them as they both contemplated the new situation.

They arrived at her door. She took out her keys and turned to say goodnight.

Michael steeled himself into action. He took a deep breath. *Here goes nothing.*

He had to stand on tiptoe to look into her eyes. He cupped her face with his hands and, oh so gently, stroked her skin with his thumbs.

Her face was as smooth as it looked. She closed her eyes. He kissed her eyelids left to right, then both sides of her mouth. Her lips were soft and warm. He kissed her again and again, just brushing the skin, then slowly pulled away. She just stood there, eyes closed.

"G'night," he said.

Her eyes fluttered open. "You're my favorite Yank, boyo." She opened the door and gave a little wave before she went in.

CHAPTER TWENTY-SIX

SKATEBOARD PARK,
DUBLIN
TWO DAYS LATER

Michael was tired but happy. The afternoon skateboarding with the guys had been a smashing success. He had given a couple lessons to riders who appreciated his attention. All was good with the world. Almost.

"Will you be here tomorrow?" Nate asked.

Michael shook his head. "I want to go fishing again. Would you like to go with me?"

"Skipping Mass, are we?" Nate asked with a grin.

"Early Mass, then fishing."

"Sorry, mate. I'd go with you, but I have to work. Me da has a job helping a chap move and needs me. Sure, and you'll find somebody else to go with ya."

I know just the person. But will she go?

He rode the bus to Eddington, determined to try once again to get Ciara to go fishing. *It would be good for her to get out of town. She needs a break. We could speak Spanish on the trip ... what else could I use?* He practiced his approach and his responses to her possible objections over and over until the bus arrived at the stop nearest the Lamb and Child pub.

He paused at the front door and took a deep breath before he could bring himself to pull it open.

Michael recognized the bartender as the man who was there when Michael had his fight with Séamus' big brother. The bartender gave him a friendly wave. "How are you today, laddie? Nice to see you again."

"Fine, fine, thanks." Michael's eyes swept the main rooms. No Ciara.

"Can I get you anything to drink? It's on the house, mate."

"Uh, no thanks. Is Ciara here? I thought she was working this afternoon."

The bartender smiled a knowing smile. "And I thought you were here to have a chat with me." He laughed. "I must tell you, laddie, how disappointed it is that I am."

He pointed toward the back room. "There she is, coming this way."

Michael turned and there she was. He felt his breath shorten.

Ciara's face lit up as she glided towards him. "Hello, Michael. I thought you were to be with the lads at the skateboard park today."

"I was." He heard his own voice waver and could feel his confidence slipping away. "Listen, do you have a minute to talk?"

She gave him a strange look that Michael couldn't quite interpret. "Yes, but just a minute. I've got customers to care for, haven't I now?"

The bartender moved a discreet distance away, allowing them some privacy.

"Uh, how's your mom?"

"She's better today, thank you. She needed some rest, that's all." Ciara moved a little closer, concern on her face. "Are you all right? Everything okay with you?"

His brain froze and he totally forgot everything he planned to say. "Hmm, well ..." His face went impossibly hot and his heart fluttered. Words came out in a rush. "Would you like to go fishing with me tomorrow?"

She stared at him for a long moment, as if perplexed that he would have the nerve to ask her out. His heart sank and he cursed himself for overstepping her boundaries.

Nice going, genius ... very smooth ... she's way out of my league. She even said she wanted nothing to do with boys ... then why did she let me hold her hand? Kiss her? ... Maybe she likes me ... oh, get serious. She wants to go to university. She doesn't have time for a boyfriend. And anyway, you're going to be leaving in about eight weeks ... Maybe she could use a short-term boyfriend ... Jesus, Michael! What kind of girl do you think she is? You're such a putz. She's a class act.

Ciara punched his arm. "Hey, Yank. Pay attention. I said sure, why not?"

CHAPTER TWENTY-SEVEN

Intercity Bus
Dublin
Sunday morning

Michael watched as Ciara dozed off. Her body slipped to her left, and her head slowly tilted until it touched the glass of the bus window. She shifted several times in her sleep, trying to find a more comfortable position. Nothing seemed to work. He reached over and gently pulled her toward him.

"Ciara, put your head on my shoulder," he said softly. "It'll be more comfortable." She didn't wake but snuggled a little closer to him. He threaded his left arm around her right one to make the fit even better. He leaned back and smiled. The only thing that would make this almost perfect position perfect would be if she had done it on her own.

Michael sat absolutely still, determined not to move even if his entire left side went numb. She was exhausted and needed to rest. He was pleased that he had broken her work-study-work cycle.

Ciara, breathing softly, moved occasionally without waking as the bus took them out of Dublin into the lush greens of the countryside. Michael was again mesmerized by the green hues of Ireland's fields and forests stretching to the horizon.

Today's horizon was indistinct with low clouds and some threatening thunderstorms in the distance. He hoped they would hold off, but he smelled rain. He didn't mind getting wet on the river, but a cold rain would certainly dampen Ciara's enthusiasm, and he desperately wanted her to have a good time on this, her first fishing expedition.

Even if it starts pouring now, and we just turn around at Luddington, this day will go down as a success. For me, anyhow.

Now, the question is: How do I explain to this city girl, the magic of going down to a stream to watch for the twists and turns of trout swimming over the gravel in clear water? Or the majestic solitude of just being out in the country? He shook his head. *Jeez, I sound like a bad advert for a fishing guide!*

They disembarked at Luddington. Ciara insisted on a walking tour of the village.

"I've never been here. Seen pictures in the tourist books but never actually been here meself. It's supposed to be a typical Irish village, whatever that means."

"Well, then, we need to do an explore, as Winnie-the-Pooh would say," Michael said as he shouldered his backpack. "Perhaps a cup of tea at that pub yonder."

"What did you say?"

He pointed down the street. "I said tea at that pub over there."

"No, you said yonder. Is that really a word?"

He made a little bow. "*Mi amiga*, thanks to my father and grandfather, I am also fluent in Air Force-speak. As in 'off we go into the wild blue yonder?'"

She looked puzzled. "I must be still a little asleep. I don't get it."

He shook his head. *Civilians.* "Okay. Yonder is also a southern expression, like from Texas. I use it on occasion, and this trip is an occasion."

"But you're not from the South. You're from New Mexico."

"Yes, but New Mexico is infested with Texans and they say yonder a lot."

After tea and scones with clotted cream graciously served by a lovely older woman who doted on Ciara, they grabbed a local taxi for the drive to the mile marker and path to the river. Michael paid the cabbie and arranged for a pick-up in four hours.

As the cabbie pulled away, Michael stood still, taking a moment to let the environment sink in. He had never before seen so many hues of green at one time. Green things growing on green things. The highlands in the distance added depth and texture to the vista. He glanced at Ciara to gauge her reaction to this idyllic setting. She stood silhouetted against the backdrop of the Irish lowlands, the wide-open, lush fields pitted with lichen-covered boulders and graced with a vast forest. She wore a dark brown cloak with a hood and a brown and green wool scarf, her long red hair blowing about in the wind. He could imagine her Irish ancestors.

"Ciara, you look like a Druid princess."

"Aye," she said in a fierce voice. "And I'll have your heart now, boyo."

You already have my heart, lass!

He desperately wanted to tell her that. Instead, he again shouldered his backpack, handed her the rod tube, and plunged into the dense forest where they were quickly swallowed up by the vegetation. After a few steps, all human signs were erased—insects flew by and leaves rustled in the breeze. The earthy scent of the river ecosystem surrounded them, different from the piñon and pine forests of northern New Mexico but having the same effect on Michael. Trout didn't live in ugly places in America. Neither did Irish trout.

Today's going to be epic!

CHAPTER TWENTY-EIGHT

NEAR LUDDINGTON
RIVER BOYNE

"This is a carbon fiber pole," said Michael. "It's a four weight and seven-and-a-half feet long. I like it because I get more action with smaller fish that we have in New Mexican mountain streams."

He gave the pole a few flicks to demonstrate the rod's flexibility, then looked up to see Ciara's face as her enthusiasm seemed to drain away.

Maybe the best thing is to let her experience it herself.

"Sorry. I could talk about fishing for hours, but I'll spare you the agony. Let's just fish, and you'll either get it or not."

"Thank you very much. Sounds like a challenge."

"Here's your pole. I'm going to show you how to cast and then we'll start. Okay?"

She smiled. "Okay."

Three hours and six trout later, Michael watched as Ciara stood on the riverbank and carefully made a cast under a willow branch. The fishing had been good, which he chose to regard as a positive omen.

Ciara was a natural. More important, she got it. She seemed to fit in the outdoors and the whole fly-fishing experience. He watched her, a picture of concentration, as she stalked a trout hiding in a deep hole a little upstream.

Michael saw a fish rise to take her fly off the water's surface. "Got him!" her joyous voice rang out. She netted the fish with newfound skill and released it back into the stream.

He slid his arm around her. "Well done. You look like you belong on the water."

She leaned into him and sighed deeply. "I can't believe how peaceful and picturesque this is. It's wonderful out here, so different from my life in Dublin." Trying not to poke him with the pole, she wrapped her arms around him and kissed him gently. Then again, harder this time.

Michael felt nearly intoxicated. *Ohmygoshthisisunbelievable!*

Breaking apart, she laughed. "You are something, Michael Anthony Callahan. An expert fishing guide on top of all your other talents."

"Ciara, do you always get amorous when you go fishing?"

"Don't know. Never been fishing before, remember? Take me fishing again, and I'll tell you." She chuckled. "Maybe it's just that a certain Yank angler turns me on. Never felt that way before, either."

Michael held her close as they stood at the edge of the river, locked together, staring into each other's eyes.

"I must smell something terrible," she said.

"Not to me you don't."

"But you like fish."

"Yes, and I like you, too."

She smiled. "That was exactly the right thing to say." And she kissed him again. Her lips were cool and unbelievably soft. She gave him a brief, ever so brief, flick of tongue.

After a moment, Michael said, "Not that I'm complaining, but I thought you said that sounded disgusting."

"Oh, I meant with Irish blokes. I thought it might be different with you, Yank."

He smiled. "For the first time in my life, I'm glad I'm not Irish."

"Me, too," she said, voice soft. "It seems that I prefer Native South American men, perhaps with just a dash of international culture."

Raindrops announced the arrival of the rains that had threatened all morning, first a patter, then a torrent. As the storm hit with the ferocity of a grizzly bear, they dashed for cover. Soaked, laughing, they huddled together under the oak trees, wrapped in his plaid ground cloth.

Her face was close to his, water dripping off her nose and chin. She laughed. "You sure know how to show a girl a good time!"

The sky exploded in a mighty thunderclap so close they could feel it. The rain transformed into pebble-sized hail like some giant hand had flipped a switch. Instinctively, Michael rolled on top of her. Hailstones pounded his back.

"Whoa, what are you doing, Michael?"

He stopped. "Sorry. I didn't mean to startle you. I was just trying to protect you from the hail." He started to slide away.

"Well," she said, "as long as you're just protecting me," and kissed him again.

He ignored the hail hammering his body and returned her kiss. Her mouth welcomed his tongue. His hand slid across her back and shoulder. He could feel her muscles through her jumper.

Ciara whispered in his ear. "I think it's better that we fished as long as we did. I'm not sure I could have resisted you, Michael Anthony Callahan. You are truly one-of-a-kind."

"Are you cold?" he asked, staring into those mesmerizing blue eyes from close range.

She shook her head. "Actually, I'm quite warm. Why do you ask?"

"I was reading the Internet about redheads. You're supposed to be more sensitive to heat and cold."

"So, you've been investigating me, have we?"

"Yeah, redheads are only about two per cent of the world's population overall but about ten per cent in Ireland."

"You know about the MC1R gene mutation that all of us redheads have?"

"I don't mind." He chuckled. "It's a nice mutation."

She nibbled on his ear. "And you know that redheads are rumored to be more passionate?"

Uncertain now, Michael answered in a slow voice. "Yeah … I think that's what one article said."

She used her nose to caress his and stroked his back. "I've never done this before. How am I doing so far?"

BOOM!

He jerked upright. "What was that?"

"We Irish call it thunder," she said and pulled his face back to hers and kissed him, her tongue exploring his mouth.

Crash!

The wind whipped through the tress, leaves and debris blew by, and the temperature dropped.

"It's going to rain like crazy," he said.

"This is Ireland. Of course, it's going to rain." She pulled him closer and wrapped her arms around him. "Stop talking so much."

BOOM!

The rain pounded down all around them. Ciara giggled. "It is distracting, isn't it?"

They slowly untangled themselves and lay side-by-side under the ground cloth. Michael stroked her cheek. "I thought you didn't like me."

"I fancied you from the start, *boyo*. Didn't want to, tried to hide it, but *ipso facto*, there you have it."

"You sure fooled me. I thought that all you wanted was to be friends."

"It is. I mean, it was. I said I don't have time for dating, and I meant it until you came along and knocked me over, you evil boy."

"Who, me?"

She edged as close as she could get and nuzzled his neck. "Yes," she breathed. "You."

CHAPTER TWENTY-NINE

WAREHOUSE DISTRICT
DUBLIN

Andropov sat at an ornate and over-sized bench he had built in his warehouse in order for him to more comfortably survey his latest array of icons. Outside, it was a cold, gray day, not far from rain. Inside, the room was warm, strains of Tchaikovsky played softly from hidden speakers, and the table in front of him sparkled with the cream of another shipment from Mother Russia. He was alone with his treasures.

As usual, the sight of so much history overwhelmed him. Where have these precious works been for the past four hundred years? What journey had they been on? Some may have been handled by Catherine the Great, or captured by Napoleon, or looted by the Germans in WW II. And the adventures they may have experienced while escaping or being hidden away from the invaders! The historian in him was fascinated by the twists and turns of mankind's story through the ages.

He slipped on a pair of gloves and picked up a small 17th century icon with a brilliant gilded frame. "Where have you been all my life, beautiful?" he asked. His finger traced a slice in the frame. "How did you get this injury? Was it from a soldier's sword? Or a lover's dagger? A careless servant?" He examined the icon from all angles, all the while caressing the frame. Then, he carefully placed it in a safe spot on the table. He picked up piece after piece, assessing each with a combination of professional and artisan eyes.

Finally, he couldn't avoid the task at hand any longer. He ripped off his gloves and threw them at the wall. He snatched up some papers and read them again. His Russian patrons had presented him with a new business plan built on the existing one that Andropov was so familiar with. "You greedy pigs," he muttered.

The new plan relegated his beloved icons to second priority. Andropov considered himself not a smuggler, not a criminal, but an art lover assisting fellow art lovers worldwide in realizing their dreams of owning magnificent *objects d'art*. He understood the attraction of the new plan for his Russian mentors. There would be new markets and fantastic profits. Nevertheless, he had voiced his concerns. And the papers in his hands told him in no uncertain terms to proceed as requested.

Andropov knew better than to object twice. Oligarchs have razor-sharp minds for business and a thin veneer of civilized behavior that could evaporate in an instant when angered, revealing their violent core. They do not argue. He had heard the rumors about what happened to people who tried. He liked his life and his lifestyle and wanted to keep both intact.

"Pigs," he said again, louder this time. "Alright, I'll make it happen. I'll stamp this program with my own brand. I'll make you richer. And me, too." He knew the numbers all made sense. Human trafficking was currently the fastest growing criminal market segment in the world.

The money was incredible. True, the risks were higher but so were the rewards.

He walked a narrow path with the oligarchs—he needed to perform well enough to be valued and paid accordingly, but he had to be careful not to become indispensable ... or expendable. It was a bit like riding a tiger—exhilarating but the dismount was a bit tricky and had to be done just right or risk being eaten by the beast.

Now, he was faced with a bit too much success. He had made overtures to his natural market for icons—Italy. The Italians loved icons as well as classic antique jewelry and *majolica*, the gorgeous tin-glazed pottery from the Renaissance. His Italian mafia contacts had been enthusiastic about the new source for women and had requested movement of the goods so quick that Andropov suspected the ideas had originated in Italy rather than Russia. Mafia dons, like Russian oligarchs, did not like delays or to be kept waiting. Consequently, Andropov was scrambling to sketch out an efficient delivery system.

However, he had a more immediate concern: he was coming down with the flu. His symptoms were beginning to pile up, and he knew from experience that when it hit him, he would topple like an oak tree in a hurricane and be useless for a week. He detested being ill and was a terrible patient. Life was difficult enough with a bad leg. He desperately wanted to close this deal, get at least one shipment completed, then nature could claim him as a victim for a week or so. It was both a blessing and a curse that he was a micro-manager and liked being in charge. He did not want to give his mentors a reason—or excuse—to gift him with an assistant. Assistants too often grew ambitious. The Russians he had working for him were fine—loyal and not very bright.

In the meantime, he washed down vitamin C tablets with what seemed like gallons of Echinacea tea, something the Irish in him found revolting. Tea should be black, strong, and served with milk, not green and weak.

The race was on—would he be able to get a deal together before he crashed and incurred the anger of both his oligarch mentors and mafia connections? He swallowed another vitamin C tablet and re-filled his teacup. He would make this work somehow.

CHAPTER THIRTY

THE LAMB AND CHILD PUB
EDDINGTON

Michael clambered out of the bus and glanced up at the gray sky, hoping the rain would hold off for a few more hours. He shouldered his backpack and stepped onto his skateboard to ride the two blocks to The Lamb and Child. According to Ciara, the pub was famous for its traditional Irish pub lunches. *Getting three birds today. Get to see Ciara, get fed at the pub, then an afternoon riding at the skateboard park. Couldn't be better.*

When he opened the massive doors and stepped inside, a rich aroma of hearty food nearly knocked him over and brought a big smile to his face. It smelled homey and delicious. Just what he needed in this still-foreign land of St. George's cafeteria food.

He spotted Ciara across the bustling, crowded front room. She looked good, wearing leggings and a blue tunic that matched her eyes, hair braided in a style he hadn't yet seen on her. The whole package was perfect. She flashed him one of her smiles and pointed to a small table against the window that sported a "Reserved" placard. *Oh yeah. VIP treatment for me!*

He slid into a chair and waited patiently for her to finish with her other customers, then to present him with a menu and another smile.

"Any specials today, *chica*?"

"*Sí, señor*, quite a few. For your dining experience today, we have your choice of Irish coddle, colcannon, Hunter's pie, champ, or boxty."

"Could you say all that again, please? Slowly."

Ciara repeated the strange list, pausing dramatically after each syllable, as if Michael were brain dead. "Now, what is your pleasure, sir?"

"No idea. I didn't understand half of what you said."

She stepped closer, hands on hips. "You did, too! You understand me fine at school."

He leaned back into his chair and smiled up at her. "I think I'll just sit here and compose some flash fiction that I'll post tonight on the Internet. The title should be something like, 'Adventures of an American Student in Ireland,' subtitled 'How I Nearly Starved to Death While Trying to Order a Meal.'"

"You cheeky sod!" She laughed. "But I guess the same would happen to me if I visited Taos."

"Not a chance! People would cluster around you like flies on a cow pie, enchanted by your accent, and making side bets on what you just said."

"No matter," she said, a touch of sadness creeping into her voice. "There's no way I'll ever get to Taos anyway."

Michael said, "I understand you fine. It's the actual dishes that I don't know. You pick one, just make sure that it has potatoes in it. I'm from Bolivia, you know. We invented potatoes."

"We Irish perfected them, boyo."

"And some iced tea, please."

"We don't have iced tea. Not on the menu. It's barbaric."

"Really?" he said. "I certainly wouldn't want you to do anything barbaric." He paused for a moment. "But do you have any ice?"

She nodded. "Of course."

"And you have tea, I assume."

"Yes," she said, exasperated. "This is Ireland."

"How 'bout you put six or eight ice cubes in a glass, then fill the glass with tea. You can call it anything you want."

"You are a cheeky sod, boyo," she said with a grin. "I'll bring you something that you'll like." She leaned in closer. "Just go easy on the onions, matey. I get off in an hour," she said with a wink.

Man, oh man, this is going to be a great day!

After devouring the Lamb and Child's version of boxty, a clever layering of potato pancakes filled with chicken, cheese, and bacon, topped with chopped tomatoes and garnished with a sauce and lightly sprinkled chopped green onions, all of which reminded Michael of an Irish quesadilla, he paid the bill and added a sizable tip. Minutes later, an annoyed Ciara appeared at his table and handed him back the tip, told him that she was through for the day, and escorted him outside and around to the pub's car park.

"I don't want your money," she said. She smiled and kissed him lightly on the cheek. "But thank you for the gesture."

"I have a surprise for you," she said and led him around the corner. "Look!" She pointed to a battered blue Vespa tucked out of the way. "It's me da's scooter. Me mum says it's mine now. And I got me license yesterday!"

Michael looked at her, excitement written all over her face and remembered how elated he felt when his parents bought him his first truck, especially the feeling of newfound independence. "Wow! That's great. This is a wonderful surprise." He bent down to examine the machine, running his hand over the leather seat.

"It's not much to look at, but it's mine," she said. "And it was his. I can remember seeing him drive it." She paused. "He died six years ago. From *haemochromatosis* which gave him cirrhosis. Hereditary, common in Celtic people—sometimes called the Celtic disease." She glanced over at Michael. "I've been tested. I don't have the condition, and I'm not a carrier."

Ciara was silent for some moments. "People say bad things about me da, that he was a drunk because couldn't hold a job, that he had cirrhosis, when in fact he was ill from something he couldn't control, something that couldn't be cured," she said, a catch in her voice. "But he was always kind to me. He would call me 'Ciara, me darlin' and hold me in his big strong arms."

She wiped her eyes and forced a smile. "He wouldn't want me to stand around in mourning, would he now? Not when there's a handsome lad nearby to impress with me driving skills." She pointed to the scooter. "Put on your skateboard helmet and hop on, boyo. I'll take us to the park."

CHAPTER THIRTY-ONE

SKATEBOARD PARK
DUBLIN

Michael held on as Ciara sliced through traffic and brought them to the skateboard park in a mind-numbing display of urban driving. The holding on was the best part of the trip.

As she parked the scooter and secured her helmet, he looked up at the thick clouds. "Rats. It looks like rain again."

"This is Ireland, boyo. Rain is never very far away." She surveyed the park. "So, this is where you spend most of your waking hours."

They heard a shout, "Hey, Yank!"

Michael waved as Nate rolled up. "Ciara, this is my friend, Nate Chismar." As the others joined them, he said, "And this is everybody else. Everybody, this is Ciara."

"All I hear from this Yank is 'skateboard, skateboard, gotta go skateboard,'" she said with a smile. "Is he really any good?"

Nate looked at Michael, then back to Ciara. "Don't really know how he stacks up with the professionals. But he's the best we've ever seen in person. So you ride?"

"No. But as my American friend here would say, 'I'm fixin' to learn.'"

"Oh my, Ciara, your accent," said Nate in mock horror. "You've been spending way too much time with the Yank."

"Not possible." Ciara smiled and turned to Michael. "I want to see you ride."

"Ciara—"

"I want to see you ride," she said again with some emphasis. "You came here to ride. So, ride."

Michael knew better than to argue. He suited up. Exhibitions had never been his thing. Competitions, yes. Exhibitions, no. He took his time and did his standard warmups to loosen his still-questionable leg. Ciara studied his moves with approval on her face.

He skated to the lip of the bowl, stood with his left foot on his board visualizing his first few hits, took a deep breath, and dropped in.

First, a couple 180s, a handstand, and a quick flip, then he let it loose. The exhilaration returned as it always did. He was free and flying in his own world. A tweaked out big air. Then another. All good. Another flip, a 360 underflip, back down into the bowl, and into a big spin. Blunt stop. He spotted the rail beckoning, calling to him. He rolled in and hit it perfectly. Stuck the landing. No pain! He thrust his arms upwards in triumph. *Yeah!* Then, he remembered Ciara and the others.

He looked up. She was standing with Nate, the other boys and girls clustered around them. She gave him two thumbs up and a big smile as he skated closer.

"All right then," she said. "I guess I'll let you teach me some of them tricks, boyo!" She hugged him and whispered in his ear, "You are amazing, Michael Anthony Callahan."

He knew he was the envy of every boy there.

"Let's get you suited up." He handed her his protective pads, then they began with the basics: which foot did she naturally put forward; how to stand on the board; how to push the board; how to stop; how to turn. An accomplished athlete, Ciara caught on quickly. All was going better than Michael had ever hoped for until, of course, it started pouring rain.

They followed Nate as the crew ran down the alley, Michael on foot, Ciara on her scooter.

Nate waved them into the club hideout where everybody shook off the rain. He stood in the room's center and addressed Ciara. "I suppose your Yank here has told you about our little club secret, hasn't he now?"

Ciara looked at Michael, then said, "I have no idea what you're talking about, Nathan."

"Ooh, very good, Michael," said Nate. "I'm surprised. You must be quite the Sphinx. If Ciara were my girlfriend, I'd tell her anything and everything."

"You said it was a secret!" Michael protested.

"And so it is." Nate locked eyes with Ciara. "And we'd like to keep it that way. Okay by you?"

She nodded.

He opened the wardrobe. "I promised your fella here a visit to the tunnels. Since you're a close personal friend of his, I reckon you can be trusted."

He handed her a torch and led the two of them down into the tunnels. "Watch your heads," he cautioned.

"This is brilliant," she breathed, flashing the beam from her torch down into the pitch-black tunnel. "I've heard about these tunnels all me life but never been in one."

"You ain't seen nothin' yet."

They entered what looked like a different world. Low ceilings and brick walls stretched into the darkness. The air was damp and musty. Some of the walls were rough and dirty, some whitewashed, some showing signs of water damage. The vaulted tunnels averaged about six feet high and about four to five feet wide in most places.

"Some of these tunnels are hundreds of years old," said Nate.

"Man, it's dark," said Michael. "Totally dark. It's like we're in a bubble of light with our torches."

"Gotta be careful where you step, especially when it rains. Most of the tunnels are pretty dry. Sometimes the water seeps in a foot or two feet deep, but sometimes there's so much water that you need to swim in a few of the tunnels. We don't go there but the City has special teams of divers who do."

The tunnels stretched ahead as far as their lights could penetrate. Occasionally, light leaked in from an opening. Michael saw pipes along one wall. "People really use these tunnels?"

"Some buildings up on the streets use tunnels for storage. They're even a couple pubs in the tunnels. Did you notice the indentations along the tunnel walls, the ones bricked up?"

"Yeah, I wondered about those. What are they for?"

"They're more tunnels branching off. Don't know where they go or what's behind them."

"Kinda spooky," Ciara said.

"Very Edgar Allan Poe," Michael said.

"*The Cask of Amontillado*," Nate replied. "Yeah, yeah. I know about the story. You and your fancy pants school. Think you know everything. Some of the rest of us unwashed types can read, too, ya know, can't we now?"

"Sorry. I didn't mean it like that," Michael said. Just in time, he ducked under a low brick arch. The tunnel turned and narrowed, forcing them to squeeze though a jagged opening.

Michael felt oddly comfortable underground. He wondered if some of his Quechua forebears had been miners. Chances were high since mines were common in resource-rich Bolivia. The Spanish conquerors had enslaved tens of thousands, if not hundreds of thousands, of indigenous over the centuries to work in the gold and silver mines. He laughed to himself. *Or maybe I'm descended from dwarfs like in the Lord of the Rings.*

Bam! He bonked his head on an especially low tunnel arch. Dazed, he dropped to his knees in the dark. "Ow!" he said. "Jeez, that hurt!"

Nate laughed. "Pay attention, Yank. If you wore your hat with the bill in front like it's supposed to be instead of backwards, you would have had some warning, silly boy."

"Thanks for the sympathy, buddy," Michael said, rubbing his forehead as he struggled to his feet.

Ciara bent down beside him and gave him a quick kiss on the cheek as she handed him his hat. "He's right, you know."

"Okay, okay, I'll wear the hat properly if it makes you happy." She rewarded him with another kiss.

Nate started in again with his tour guide impression. "Nobody knows how many tunnels there are. At least," he conceded, "nobody who I know knows. Tunnels are supposed to be off-limits. There aren't any maps available to regular folk."

He seemed pretty confident as they moved into what was increasingly like a vast underground labyrinth to Michael. Occasionally, Nate pointed to a foundation and identified the building it belonged to: a bank, a pub, a church.

"How do you know all this?" asked Michael.

"It's sort of a hobby of mine."

These skateboard club guys must spend a lot of time down here!

"Do you even go to school, Nate?"

"Online, bro. I'm studying for the Leaving Certificate examination next year so I can qualify for university."

"What?"

"What do you mean, what?"

"I mean … I'm surprised, that's all," Michael stammered.

"Don't go acting like some upper-class toff, Michael, me boy. Us blue-collar types have hopes and dreams, too. Just like real people."

"Which way are we going now?" Ciara asked in a heroic effort to change the subject.

"Out by the River Liffey," Nate said. "A place where it starts getting wide enough for ships. It's one of my favorite spots."

They could barely make out a tiny dot in the distance, which grew larger as Nate led them forward to a low opening they had to crawl through. He pushed aside some boards and brush that hid the opening, and they crawled out onto a grassy ledge. All three stood upright and stretched to work out the kinks. The sky was still gray but looked marvelous after their being underground for so long.

They had a spectacular view up the Liffey as it opened toward the ocean, large ships visible in the distance. Now that the rain had stopped, wisps of sea fog rolled in over the rough water.

"What do ya think, Ciara?" asked Nate.

"Oh, I can see Granny O'Malley sailing into Dublin, blasting through the fog, flags flying."

"More like Viking ships full of soldiers ready to launch raids inland."

"You have your fantasies, Nathan Chismar, I'll have me own."

CHAPTER THIRTY-TWO

St. George's College
Dublin

Michael stood outside Ciara's history class, waiting for her class to end. She was the last out of the door and flashed him a trademark smile.

He took her hand, and they started down the hall. "Spanish homework will have to wait. I just got a text from my mom. She wants to talk. I have to go back to my room," he explained. "And hit the Internet."

"To call her?"

"Yeah. On our family website."

"Your family has a website?" she asked. "What ever for?"

"We're scattered all over the world. Cousins, uncles, aunts, grandparents. In Australia, Italy, New Mexico, and a few other places. This way, we can video conference and keep up with each other, leave messages, post photographs. You know, family stuff."

"Not my family," she said. "Your mum wants a video conference?"

"Not for long. Exchange students are supposed to limit contact with family while we're overseas. She's pretty serious about following that policy, so this is probably some important update or something that Mom wants me to know."

Ciara went quiet.

And she waited.

And waited.

Finally, Michael got the message. "Would you like to come with me and meet my Mom?"

"Why yes, thank you, Michael." She elbowed him in the side. "Took you long enough."

They climbed the stairs into the dorms and walked down the long, carpeted hall to Michael's end room.

"Never been up here before to see how you boarders live. Very posh."

They left the door open per St. George's rules and sat in front of Michael's desk.

"Will there be any pictures of a baby Michael?"

"Ha, Ha!" *I hope not. But it would be just like Mom.*

The home page featured, appropriately enough, a home. Several homes, in fact, along with flags of the countries where they were located. Michael clicked on the American flag, then on the New Mexico flag.

"*That's* your house?"

He nodded, embarrassed.

"It's massive! Looks like a museum! How big is it?"

"Pretty big," he muttered. He didn't say that Babushka's was even larger.

She reached and moved the computer cursor to explore the house interior. "Oh my, how many people can eat at your dining room table? Looks like a banquet hall. And the walls! Your house is a blinkin' art gallery!"

"My dad collects art," he said, knowing it sounded lame. "Babushka hauls us around to art museums on holidays," as if that excused everything.

"And barns! And pastures. How many horses do you have? Ooh, look at the mountains! They're gorgeous! Your family is bloody rich, boyo."

I knew this was a bad idea. Michael re-gained control of the mouse and clicked on "video." After a few seconds, his mother's smiling face suddenly filled the screen. He thought she looked better than ever. "Hey, kiddo!" she said. "Thank you for calling on such short notice."

"Hi Mom."

Her face registered surprise. "And your friend is … ?"

"Sorry, Mom. This is Ciara, a friend from school."

"Lovely to meet you, Ciara."

"And you, Doctor Callahan."

"Quickly, son. Must be off, you know. I just needed to let you know that we're flying up for a week at Banff. The ski area is opening early this year."

Any further conversation was interrupted by a chorus of "Hey Mikey!" as two blond heads appeared and blocked their mother's face.

Michael laughed. "Hey, dudes!"

"We're going to ride in Canada this week!" said his little brother, Justin.

"Eighteen inches of fresh pow yesterday, more tomorrow!" said Justin's twin, Jeremy. "Gonna bust some moves, bro! Take the country by storm."

"Who are you?" they chorused, finally aware that Michael was not alone.

"I'm Ciara."

"Do you ride?" Justin asked.

"Horses, yes."

"No," he said, exasperated. "I mean *ride.* You know, snowboard."

"No, I'm Irish. It is genetically impossible for us to snowboard. Leprechauns freeze in the snow."

They shook their heads as if she had been speaking Klingon. "Too bad. Mikey's the best snowboarder ever," Jeremy said.

Justin said, "Only until this year, dude. While you're suffering in the flats of Ireland, we'll be upside down in the park. Double corks. Watch out!"

"Mikey's got a girlfriend!" Jeremy shouted.

"With red hair!" Justin said.

"Mikey's got a girlfriend, Mikey's got a girlfriend!" they chorused.

Michael's mother shoo'ed the twins away. They ran off, still chanting. She looked at Ciara. "Terribly sorry, Ciara." She shrugged. "Boys." She smiled again. "I didn't want to leave the country without telling you, son."

They chatted a few minutes more before she excused herself and they said their goodbyes.

After the screen went blank, Ciara turned on Michael. "Are you mad? Do you even know what you have here?"

He didn't answer.

"A family. A full family. Parents. Siblings. A house like a manor estate with grounds larger than our school's! People there who love you. Do you realize how lucky you are?" she said, shaking her head. "My mother works two, sometimes three jobs to make things work ... she is exhausted, no time for fun ... or for me ... your family can jet off to another country to ski any time it wants. Or send you to a fancy school abroad without even blinking."

"I'm not sure my dad loves me," Michael said quietly. "I think he's disappointed in me. We don't have the same goals. He wants me to do this, I want to do that. Almost by reflex."

"Of course, you don't have the same goals, boyo. You're both males and of different generations."

"The twins are more like him."

"Yes, and they're not teenagers yet. Just wait. If they are anything like what you've told me, their high school years will feature multiple explosions. It's the way it's supposed to be. Your dad says he wants you to be independent, doesn't he?"

"Yes."

"Well, he's succeeded. You are one of the most independent lads I know."

Michael protested, "But we fight all the time."

Ciara frowned. "I wish I had a dad to fight with all the time."

"My dad used to call me his number one son. He doesn't anymore."

"Why?"

"I don't know."

"What's the significance?"

"I was his number one son. Now he has three."

"So?"

"There's an Asian streak in the family—my babushka was born in Shanghai. The first son is groomed to take over the family business or affairs. It's old fashioned and distinctly not PC, but it's the way it is in much of the world. Primogeniture is the fancy word for it."

"I know what the word means, Michael," she said, annoyed. "In medieval Latin, *primogenitura* meant a first born. From the Latin root *primo* meaning at first plus *gignere*, to beget." She paused, still angry. "Seven years of Catholic school Latin, *boyo*."

Oops. "Okay, okay. Sorry." He tried a smile. "Given half a chance, I'll take any opportunity to say something completely inappropriate."

"World champion, in my mind," she sniffed. "But back to the main point. You are his first son, his number one son. That number hasn't changed with the addition of your younger brothers. And it will never change even if you do something really stupid, which is, I'm afraid, a distinct possibility given your attitude."

With that, a silence settled between them.

Ciara spoke first. "I want to do things different from me mum. I want to get out of here. She's stuck. She left school too soon, married too young, had two babies too fast, lost her husband. She wants a better future for us but can't manage to get out of the hole she dug with bad decisions."

"My family," said Michael, "or rather this family I am growing up in—I don't really think I fit in—are all over-achievers. My paternal grandfather is a major general, my grandmother is a famous artist, my maternal grandparents own a sheep station in Australia, my mother is a World Bank economist, my father is a decorated fighter pilot and worked in the White House. Even my younger brothers are over-achievers to be—super jocks and really smart. All I want to be is a snowboard instructor and coach. I want to coach in the Winter X Games and the Olympics."

She looked at him with surprise on her face. "Michael, do you hear yourself?"

"What?"

"You just said that you want to be a coach at the X Games. At the Olympics. What is not over-achiever about those ambitions?"

He struggled to find the right words. "It's not that; it's simply what I want to be."

"Which is exactly what?"

Michael didn't speak.

"You have goals, right?"

"Yes."

"You know goals without a plan are just daydreams?"

"Of course, I know that." He settled back in his chair, arms crossed. "I know exactly what I have to do to get where I need to go, the licenses, the experience, everything."

"So, you have a plan all laid out to achieve your lifetime goals?"

He nodded again.

"And you're sixteen?"

He nodded, slower this time.

"Michael, listen to what you just said. Why do you think you're not an over-achiever but the rest of your family is?"

He nearly shouted, "It's simply what I want to do! What I need to be!"

She cupped his face in her hands. "Of course, that's what you want. It's you." She kissed him lightly. "You, Michael, a boy with big dreams, determined to make the most of himself. That, my lovely, is what you are. You belong in that family. You fit. You *are* a Callahan."

He stared into Ciara's amazing blue eyes and thought for a moment. His emotions swirled. Almost light-headed, he wondered, *Could she be right?*

CHAPTER THIRTY-THREE

St. George's College

Donal Gillmore leaned heavily on his cane as he trudged through the hallway toward the administrative offices. He had a monstrous head cold coupled with flu-like symptoms; beads of sweat adorned his forehead, and he felt as miserable as he ever had. *I can't wait for the school day to end. I am going to drag myself home to bed.*

As he passed the double doors to the dining hall, he glanced inside. *There's that Harrington girl, all doe-eyed, sitting with the little American.* Gillmore watched the eye contact, the way Ciara leaned across the cafeteria table, entranced by the Yank and laughing at something he said, hanging on his every word like he was a prophet or something. If she would pay that much attention in class, she would be a champion student.

Stories about student romances flashed though the teachers' lounge weekly. Gossip really, which Gillmore abhorred, but none of the stories topped the abrupt blossoming of the high-visibility Harrington-Callahan union. Gillmore had witnessed the stolen glances and furtive touches between them, almost as if they were drug addicts needing a fix. Gilmore hadn't had a woman look at him like that since he had seduced his fiancée so long ago when he was whole, handsome, and a budding rugby star.

He did not approve of co-ed colleges—it was bad enough at university—but teenagers were simply not capable of handling hormonal surges. The American now waited for Harrington at the door of Gillmore's class every afternoon, as if to rub in the fact that he had a pass from the headmaster.

Gillmore knew he had done the right thing throwing the boy out of his class. It irritated him that the headmaster seemed to have adopted the boy. Gillmore was sure this was a deliberate move by the headmaster to embarrass him, a slight he would not forgive nor forget.

Gillmore endured his position as history teacher at St George's, even though he felt underappreciated and considered a position as a university lecturer a better fit for his self-image. He did it because it enhanced his social position without too much visibility, which was even more important to his outside interests.

Hmm … Everybody knows the uppity Miss Harrington's goal is to attend Trinity College Dublin. I think her next history paper won't be graded as high as she expects. And next year after she applies to TCD, perhaps I could have a word with a member of the admissions committee. Competition for acceptance there is so intense that a single vote of no-confidence should be sufficient to eliminate someone. Anyone whose judgment is poor enough to consort with the worst sort of American doesn't deserve to attend the TCD that I attended—

His cell phone vibrated in his jacket pocket right as he reached the Admin offices. He checked the number, muttered a curse, and stepped outside for a bit of privacy, leaning against the building wall for support.

"I told you *never* to call me here."

"It couldn't be helped, comrade. I have been talking to our Italian associates about our meeting tomorrow."

"Yes? Get on with it, I don't have much time. I'm sick, and I want to sleep."

"I told them you were sick. They said they could not wait for you to get well. They have to go back to Italy this weekend but won't meet with you while you're sick. The head guy is *takoj nikchemnij*—worthless person—more of a chair-warming accountant than an operative, afraid of a room full of germs. They want us to close the deal tomorrow."

Gillmore was vain about his negotiating abilities and customer service attitude. He knew he was a micro-manager but took pride in his skills. Plus, he had all those no-nonsense oligarchs watching him. Very closely. *Can I trust him to do this? Russians aren't really very good at negotiating with Europeans. 'Do it my way or I will shoot you' is not an acceptable Western business practice.*

"I can handle it, comrade."

Hmm. Maybe. The important details are already worked out. And the money, glorious money! It will just start pouring in! That should please the heavies back in Moscow.

Decision made, Gillmore said, "Okay. I will send you an email tonight with our last points. Make sure the Italians are happy. Stress our network capabilities and that we're always looking for ways to please them. Tell them if there's anything in particular they want, including changes to delivery dates, please let us know, et cetera. You know the drill; you've listened to me before. And if anything, and I mean anything, starts to go wrong, call me. Understood?"

"*Da,* comrade."

Gillmore smiled to himself. *I will go to bed with a hot drink and dream of where I could spend the winter holidays— close to my money hidden away in the ever-so-accommodating Estonia or lying on a beach in the Canary Islands. Such decisions!*

He pushed himself off the wall and entered the Admin offices for his appointment with the school nurse. Yes, his subordinates could handle this one meeting without his supervision.

CHAPTER THIRTY-FOUR

ST. GEORGE'S
ATHLETIC FIELDS

Michael finished his stretching routine and did a handstand in gleeful celebration. Weeks of running, stretching, and basic tumbling had strengthened his legs. At last, he no longer felt any pain. *Now to get back into parkour!* He tucked, rolled to his feet, and started looking for some obstacles to climb and jump over.

His eyes locked on Ciara as she strode toward the track and zeroed in on him. She flashed one of her thousand-watt smiles as she headed in his direction.

He watched her jaunty stride and felt his pulse race. He wondered about this lovey-dovey stuff. It was a new, confusing state of mind. Did he love her, or did he simply love the idea of being loved? She was like everything he'd ever imagined. And nothing like what he'd imagined. She was Ciara. Unique. Smashing, his mom would say. Stellar, he would say. Stellar, like Ciara. In every dictionary, the definition of the word stellar should include her picture.

She stood beside him, close enough for him to catch her scent as it washed over him. He loved it. And knew then that he loved her.

"I aced my Spanish oral exam, thanks to you, *señor*. I gave a little talk about *acequias*. They were impressed. *Muchas gracias.*"

He gave a little bow. "*De nada, señorita. Era mi placer.*"

"I'm taking you to my favorite pub in Dublin tomorrow night," she announced.

"Wait, seriously?"

"My treat. Do not say no."

"Yes'm, Lady Ciara, ma'am."

"Actually, I've only seen pictures of this place, but in my mind, it's my favorite pub in Dublin."

"What's the occasion?"

"You know … " She smiled at him, then went all shy and her face went pink. "You know," she whispered. "It'll be our two-week anniversary."

He remembered that day on the riverbank, then nodded, memories tumbling over themselves. The way it felt to hold her had surprised him—so soft yet so strong. Her athletic muscles and the smoothness of her skin, her scent, the sensations her touches had created, sensations he had never experienced before. *Ohmygoshsheisincredible!*

"And it's your Thanksgiving—okay, okay, a few weeks early. I looked it up on the school computer. I know you Yanks are all about your Thanksgiving."

"Great! I'll go with the Irish Thanksgiving menu. Corned beef and cabbage."

She punched him on the arm. "I told you, no self-respecting Irish person eats corned beef and cabbage. That is an American stereotype of us."

He laughed as he grabbed her and wrapped himself around her. "I know. And you are certainly no stereotype."

She whispered in his ear, "As are you, boyo. As are you."

They arrived at Ray O'Keefe's Pub in teenage style, Ciara weaving through traffic on her scooter and up onto the sidewalk, disdaining the valet parking. Michael was a bit disoriented from riding on the wrong side of the road, not to mention hanging on to her for dear life.

The pub, located in a former Victorian-era bank building, boasted an impressive façade, all brick and marble. Eight-foot oak and glass doors opened into an enormous foyer, topped with stunning high-arched ceilings embedded with skylights, and splashy art covered the walls. They gazed up in awe at the enormous fluted pink granite Corinthian columns topped with elaborate leafy capitals supporting the ceilings. An immense granite bar flanked by two nearly life-sized statues of toga-clad female figures holding lamps aloft dominated the entryway view.

Ciara threaded her arm through Michael's and sighed in delight. The bar itself was overshadowed by a vast pyramid of back-lit glass shelves crammed with dozens of whiskeys, vodkas, and liqueurs and topped with an enormous vase filled with dazzling flowers. A balcony jutted out over the main floor of the restaurant. It looked as though someone had squeezed a museum into a restaurant.

The place was jam-packed with well-dressed patrons—mostly old. Michael didn't see anyone under thirty except the servers. The place buzzed with chatter. Lots of chatter. The overall effect was of luxury in a high-energy environment.

"Oh my," she breathed. "It's even better than the pictures."

Michael said, "This is over-the-top!"

She squeezed his arm and gave him one of her magic smiles. "I told them this meal was a special occasion."

Michael knew then the night was going to be epic.

The maître d' led them upstairs to the balcony and seated them at a tiny table with a smashing view of the entire downstairs area. They squeezed into the small space, nearly touching the next table. Michael stole a look out of the corner of his eye, where two big men wearing expensive suits that didn't quite fit across their broad shoulders and thick chests sat across from two smaller, better-dressed men. Their table was littered with empty bottles, some wine, one clear glass, probably vodka.

Michael turned his attention back to his date. All he wanted was to stare into her eyes and maybe hold her hand across the table.

They sat back to enjoy their surroundings and each other. Their server appeared and handed each a menu. Michael ordered a bottle of chilled San Pellegrino mineral water for the table. With a smile, Ciara chose the grilled trout; Michael chose the evening special, an Indian curry.

They chatted about their surroundings, school, even a little about fishing, Ciara's new passion. Mostly they just looked at each other with silly smiles on their faces.

The server brought their dinner and presented the plates with a flourish, grin on his face. Ciara produced her phone and had him take pictures of them and the food.

Michael took his first bite. "Yeow, this curry is spicy!"

"I thought you ate lots of spicy food in New Mexico."

"True, but I'm not used to curries. Love them, though. This one could double as rocket fuel." He chuckled. "I'm going to gobble a bucket full of mints to cool my breath. Otherwise, if I'm lucky enough to get close to you tonight, I might melt your face."

"You are such a gentleman, so considerate. Maybe I should have a kiss now before you get dangerous." She rose out of her seat and leaned across the table to give him a soft kiss. "There, that's better. No melting, either." She patted her chest over her heart. "Except in here."

As they ate, the conversation from the table next to theirs started to filter through the general buzz of conversation. Michael picked up some Russian words, then Italian. One of the Russians took off his coat. He was wearing a tight short-sleeve shirt, and Michael couldn't help noticing the intricate tattoos that wove their way from his huge biceps down his thick forearms to his hands. *Oh no! What are they doing here?*

He tried to concentrate on Ciara, who was busy taking in the atmosphere, but he kept one ear tuned to the neighboring table conversation, which grew louder now that there were a couple more empty bottles. *Oh my, are they talking about what I think they are? No way! They must be really drunk if they think they're safe speaking in foreign languages here.*

Michael cupped his hands over his face to concentrate on the conversation. He looked up. Ciara was staring at him, a strange look on her face.

Suddenly, the men shook hands and staggered to their feet to leave.

He waited until they were halfway down the stairs. "Ciara, stay here."

"Michael?"

He threw some euros on the table, then strode across the main floor, trying to squeeze through the tables as fast as he could without looking conspicuous. A waiter opened the door for him and he stepped outside right as the valet delivered the Russians' vehicle, a black Mercedes G-Class SUV. He watched as it pulled away from the door, then stopped, waiting to inch its way into the evening traffic.

Michael turned to run back into the pub and almost crashed into Ciara. "We need to get out of here."

"What's going on, boyo?"

"Not here." He pulled her away from the crowd around the door.

"Those guys are organized crime. The big ones are Russian. The other guys, Italians. They're planning a big joint operation here in Dublin."

She shook her head. "You're havin' me on. Since when do you speak Russian?"

"Since I was a baby. My whole family speaks Russian at home. Ciara, listen. This is important! Trust me!"

"Russian organized crime. Here?" Ciara said. "I have a hard time with that, boyo."

"Remember when that big guy took off his jacket?"

She nodded. "So?"

"The tattoos. They were Russian prison tattoos—totally different from any other kind of tats. And I heard them talking. They're smuggling icons now."

"So? This is Ireland. We have a long history of smuggling."

"Icons are just the easy part, Ciara. The Italians want girls, teenagers, for prostitution. Right now. And the Russians agreed to use their smuggling network. There's lots of money in human trafficking. It's a dirty business."

"How do you know this?"

"Last semester, two girls in my class in Taos cut school, hitchhiked to Santa Fe, and went shopping. They were kidnapped at a mall, pumped full of drugs, and sold to pimps. They were raped repeatedly every night for a month before being rescued." Michael ran his hands through his hair, despairing. "If these guys aren't stopped, the girls they bring through Dublin will end up the same way—enslaved and prostituted."

Ciara opened, then closed her mouth as she struggled with what was happening. "Are you sure?"

He took a deep breath. "Yes."

"Positive?"

"Yes!"

"Girls, Michael? Girls like me?"

He nodded.

Her eyes narrowed. She clenched her jaw and morphed into an angry Irish warrior. "What do we do?"

"We have to have proof. Follow them. Then, call the Garda, let them handle it. But we need to follow these guys now before they get away. Otherwise we're just a couple loony teenagers with a crazy, unbelievable story."

"This does not sound like one of your better ideas, Michael. Those blokes were huge, like cyborgs or bridge trolls or something. Dangerous doesn't even begin to describe them."

"I don't know what else to do." His heart pounded in his chest. He forced himself to stand still for a moment to calm down. "You go home. I'll follow them. Alone."

She stared at him a moment. "Are you serious? If you're in, I'm in."

"You need to work on your survival instincts, Ciara. You're right. This is going to be dangerous."

"And how do you plan to follow them, Mister Wild West Indian tracker? On foot?"

Yipes, she's right!

"Not likely, boyo. I have the scooter."

"No," Michael said. "No way. It's too dangerous."

"Why? Because I'm a girl?"

He shook his head, then said in a quiet voice, "No, because I'm in love with you and don't want to see you get hurt."

She reached over and touched his cheek. "We'll discuss that later." She pointed to the scooter. "Get on."

He slammed on his helmet and swung in behind Ciara as she launched down the street. Michael clutched her tight and tried to hold on as they shot like an arrow into the night. Streetlamps flashed by. She wove through the almost stationary heavy evening traffic.

"It's a black Mercedes SUV," he shouted next to her ear. "Big boxy thing."

The little scooter sounded like the throbbing engine was about to explode. She cranked it, doing things its designers hadn't even considered. She was all in. *When this girl decides to do something, she frickin' does it!*

Everything was a blur. They raced in and out of the main traffic flow through the city centre, flying blind, looking for the Mercedes.

"There!" shouted Michael. "Two blocks. It's turning right."

"Got it." She cranked the throttle, then had to brake to avoid a car. They skidded, and she almost lost it. She glanced over her shoulder, then blasted away from the danger. She had to slot into traffic for a right turn. Horns blared as she cut off a truck, then a car. She leaned into the turn. Around the corner. There was the Mercedes, stuck behind a delivery truck blocking the street. About five vehicles separated them.

"Slow down," he said. "Follow at a distance. Try to get their license number." Relaxing a bit, Michael felt the adrenaline ebb away. His pounding heart slowed as his breathing ramped down to almost normal. He squeezed Ciara's midsection. "You were great!"

She shrugged like it was no big deal. Like cheating death on this pipsqueak scooter was a normal, everyday thing.

CHAPTER THIRTY-FIVE

Dublin

The delivery truck driver finally pried the vehicle from its awkward position and moved enough to open space on the other side of the street.

The impatient Mercedes driver squeezed past, bumped up on the sidewalk, back onto the roadway, and disappeared around the corner. The five other cars in front of the scooter stayed put.

"Go!" Michael said.

Ciara gunned the motor and wove a path around and between the motionless cars, onto the sidewalk, then followed around the corner. Michael caught a glimpse of the Mercedes' taillights as it shot down the street and plunged into evening traffic heading northeast. He pointed. "There!" Ciara nodded and increased her speed. She stayed three cars back, far enough to hide behind the other vehicles, close enough to not lose the quarry.

The Mercedes passed through some of the nicest sections of Dublin that Michael had ever seen, well-lit and bustling. Dubliners were out in force in the cool but pleasant evening air, filling the streets. The SUV slid into the elaborate entrance to one of Dublin's largest and most expensive hotels and braked under the portico. Ciara passed the hotel, crossed over to the opposite side of the street, up on the sidewalk, and reversed to hide behind a parked truck.

"Did you get the license number?" she asked as they watched the valets approach the Mercedes.

"Yes." He leaned forward and spoke into her ear, then made her repeat the combination of numbers and letters twice. He patted her leg. "Excellent." He dug into his jacket for his phone, entered the license number in Messages for backup, then stuffed it away again. "Now, let's stay on those guys."

Car doors were flung open, and all four men staggered out of the SUV. They exchanged drunken hugs and handshakes. The smaller men, identified by Michael as the Italians, waved good-bye and entered the hotel. The Russians clambered back into their car and slid into the evening traffic.

After three cars passed, Ciara turned the scooter and rolled in behind the Russians as they wove their way into the Port of Dublin warehouse district, then the old port district. Buildings quickly became less well cared for, more rundown, the streets darker and narrower.

She maintained her distance until at one street crossing, the Mercedes raced ahead of the light and through the intersection well after it turned red. Ciara and the two cars ahead of her glided to a stop. She pounded her fist on her handlebars and growled something in Irish.

Michael leaned forward. "It's okay. We're doing the best we can. Just follow in that general direction, and we'll try to pick them up again. Those taillights are unique."

She muttered something Irish again, then timed the green light, and sped around the slow-moving cars blocking their way. They headed deeper into the dark port area.

No Mercedes. Only a few dilapidated delivery trucks parked at random intervals.

"We need to be systematic about this," he said, leaning forward to speak in her ear. "Cruise the area. Come in from a different direction each time. That way we won't look like we're following anybody. We'll look like a couple kids just out cruising, breaking our family curfew or something, or just plain lost."

"Easy to do, boyo, 'cause that's what we are. Lost."

They made several passes through the area. Off in the distance, they saw lights come on in a dark warehouse. Ciara turned the block before the warehouse, swung out to the left, and headed north. She hung a quick left, then two more, and came back heading east almost to the docks. Michael motioned for her to stop. She pulled into a vacant lot and they dismounted. He waved his hand. "They're somewhere over there. Close, too."

"Why did they do that kind of business in a pub, of all places?"

He shrugged. "Dunno."

She stared at him. "It was pretty noisy, though. And they were getting drunker by the minute."

"We were probably the only people in the pub who could even hear, much less understand, them."

"And you were probably the only person in Ireland who could decipher their words."

Lucky me.

Ciara seemed to remember something. Hands on hips, she faced him down. "And why did it take Russian criminals lurking around for you to tell me that you spoke Russian, boyo?"

Oops.

"You and your secrets!" She looked as if she was about to get angry, then she must have remembered something else because her stance softened. She moved in close. "Tomorrow, me darlin' boy, we'll discuss all your secrets along with that other thing you said to me earlier." She kissed him, ran her fingers through his hair, and stepped back, smiling. "Whew, you are something, boyo. Full of surprises!" Then, her face changed, and she was all business. "What should we do now?"

Decision time, Michael me boy. "You go six blocks that way, park, and wait. Give me twenty minutes. If I'm not there by then, go home. Get safe."

"Are you kidding me? You're going to follow them? Alone? On foot? Do you remember the size of those blokes? They've been on steroids since birth and you want to mess with them? What kind of drugs are you on, Michael?"

"Twenty minutes," he said again. "I will be back in twenty minutes." He hooked his helmet onto the bike.

"You come back to me, Michael Callahan." She hugged him, then swung her leg over the seat and raced away.

He headed in the general direction of the warehouse lights, now hidden in the shadows behind two other structures. He didn't have the foggiest idea of what to do. This was what his father would call a surveillance operation.

The task wasn't too complicated. The basic plan was to simply follow one or more of the Russians to wherever they hid the items being smuggled—icons, guns, or girls, then call the authorities. And convince someone to do something. The tricky bit right now was not to get caught.

Not a sophisticated plan by any means. Michael shrugged. He had only read about this kind of stuff. The Callahans had a massive family library. His father even had an Academy buddy in Angel Fire, a retired lieutenant colonel, who wrote thrillers and was a frequent dinner guest at the Callahan hacienda where they discussed and dissected best-sellers. Michael decided to employ techniques learned from fictional CIA, Mossad, and special operations characters.

He drifted along, trying desperately to be invisible. He used his small size to stay low and, he hoped, inconspicuous.

Sound carried well through the narrow alleyways, allowing him to hear, with a minimum of attention, every noise. Too many noises. Michael was a small town boy, not used to the sounds of a port city and had difficulty sorting and sifting through them for danger signals.

And it was dark. Really, really dark. Dark enough to conjure up every horror movie he'd ever seen, especially the ones where some stupid teenagers all keep going into the night instead of turning around, totally oblivious to the madman with a chainsaw or a knife or an axe waiting around the corner.

His heart hammered against his ribs. His hands shook. His emotions roiled his entire body and threatened to clog his brain. He concentrated on moving quietly to help settle his fear.

There! Off to the right. Lights came on in a warehouse on a corner down the street. He struggled to get his breathing under control—in his mind, his breathing echoed in the night like a stallion after a long gallop. Sweat trickled down his spine. He crept closer.

Michael heard voices around the corner. Russian men! He stood still for a moment, too terrified to move. He reversed his direction and moved carefully back down the alley. He turned at the corner and started running for his life, imagining shouts and shots and dozens of ways to die.

CHAPTER THIRTY-SIX

WAREHOUSE DISTRICT

Michael paced around and around the scooter, hands on his head, chin down. He wanted to scream in frustration. Ciara stood to one side, waiting for him to speak.

"I have to go back," he said.

"Michael, don't be a fool! They might see you this time."

"I have to go back." He knew he was only being stubborn. "I screwed up. I panicked. I need to see what is going on in that warehouse. Otherwise, I'm just a teenager with an overactive imagination. I'll be laughed out of the Garda station."

"Even if you get close enough to see something, there's no reason the Garda will listen any differently. Just tell the authorities and let them handle it from there."

"No," he shook his head. "If I actually see something nasty in the warehouse, I can make the Garda give me a lie detector test or something. Anything. At least I'll know for sure. Right now, I'm so wound up I don't even believe me. I couldn't convince a third grader."

Ciara's voice was soft in the dark. "You convinced me, boyo."

Michael squeezed her hand and started back toward the warehouse before she could talk him out of it.

"I'm going with you."

Startled, he turned to face her. "Are you crazy? You need to stay here."

"No. I'm not just standing here in the dark, scared out of my mind. If I'm going to be scared, I need to be doing something worthwhile."

No time to argue. Not that it would do any good. "Okay, but stay close. And quiet."

"Don't worry."

He really didn't know how to go about this urban spying. He could hear his father whispering in his ear, "Go with your strengths, kiddo." Michael paused and tried to remember the route he had taken. He stood, eyes closed, going over the plan, visualizing like he would right before a run down a slopestyle course, remembering the shadows, the turns in the street, the potholes that could trip him up, the doorways that offered some protection.

Hey, this is just like hunting! Well, something like hunting. Being stealthy, quiet, and undetected in the woods was different than in a city, but many of the principles were the same. He would become a hunter, coupled with his own visualization techniques.

Michael and Ciara made their way down the streets toward the warehouse where a few lights shone dimly through dirty windows. They stopped several times to listen for activity.

Up close, even in the dark, the warehouse looked like it was two hundred years old and hadn't had a lick of maintenance during those entire two centuries. Grime covered the stonework, the wooden windowsills had never seen a paintbrush and were rotting, the ground level windows were painted black on the inside, and all the outside metal features were pitted from the salt air. They crept along one wall toward a steel door. Michael tried the handle. Locked.

She whispered, "Aren't you going to pick the lock?"

He turned his head to look at her crouched in the darkness. "I'm sorry, Ciara," he whispered. "I haven't mastered that particular life skill."

He could see her smile even in the night. "But you will, boyo. I have faith."

"And even if this is the place, remember that there are at least two big dudes inside. Really big. Monsters."

Just then, there was a rumble from inside the building and a corrugated metal delivery door slowly opened upward. Light flooded the street and the black Mercedes roared out, turned toward them. Michael pulled Ciara into the doorway and they flattened themselves against the door. The vehicle flashed past while the heavy door closed behind it. Quiet returned to the street.

Michael looked at Ciara. Her eyes were wide open. "That was so close!" She buried her face in his shoulder and shuddered.

He hugged her tight, then pulled out his cell phone. He carefully covered the screen, called up his GPS app, and dropped a pin at their location. He whispered, "Time to go."

They retraced their steps back to the scooter, taking care to stay in all the dark spots they could find.

As they put on their helmets, Michael said, "We'll go to the Garda tomorrow after classes."

"Not tonight?"

"These guys aren't going anywhere. The afternoon will be fine. We don't need to attract any more attention."

CHAPTER THIRTY-SEVEN

GARDA SIOCHÁNA HEADQUARTERS
THE NEXT AFTERNOON

After classes, Michael and Ciara drove up to the imposing Georgian stone building that housed their local Garda headquarters, and asked the desk sergeant if they could speak with Superintendent Hallums. Michael had to insist they needed to speak directly with the Superintendent. With a shrug, the sergeant directed them to the adjacent waiting room.

As the clock ticked past an hour wait, Michael's spirits spiraled down. "I'm not feeling it about this meeting."

"What happened to my optimistic, bubbly, Yank boyfriend, boyo? Hallums has to listen. It's his duty."

Boyfriend! Wow! That's a first! Maybe the meeting won't go well, but this day is the best ever! He squeezed her hand and gave her a smile.

The sergeant called out. "Oy! Wake up over there. The super will see you now."

As they entered Hallums' spacious office, he made no attempt to greet them, nor did he offer them seats. "What is it?" he grumped.

"Thank you for seeing us, Superintendent," Michael said.

The Superintendent crossed his arms and stared, unsmiling. "What do you want?"

Michael related the events of the evening at the pub, the conversation he overheard, and the chase after the Mercedes into the warehouse district.

Hallums leaned forward in his chair. "Why should I believe any of this, this fairy tale?"

Michael handed him a sheet of paper. "We have a license number, Superintendent. And a photo of the vehicle." He showed Hallums his phone.

"So what? How do I know it's valid? It's a number, not proof."

Stay cool, Ace. You should have anticipated this. "I saw the men get into the vehicle. Four men who were conspiring to break Irish law."

"What's your proof?"

"I heard them."

Ciara spoke up. "I was there, Superintendent. I saw what was happening!"

Hallums ignored her. He stared at Michael. "I'm supposed to believe you can speak Russian?"

Michael met his stare. "Do you speak Russian, Superintendent?"

"Of course not! Hardly anyone here speaks Russian."

Michael slowly spoke several sentences of Russian questioning the marriage of the Superintendent's parents, what Michael thought of his wife's manners, and the relative and absolute stupidity of his two sons.

Hallum's only reaction was a shrug. "Okay, you speak Russian. That doesn't prove any of your story."

Michael tugged on Ciara's arm. "Thank you for hearing us out, Superintendent. Sorry for taking your time."

They stood outside the headquarters building next to Ciara's scooter.

"I guess we shouldn't be surprised," Ciara said. "Because of his sons, Sean and Séamus, there was no way we could convince the Superintendent of anything."

Michael said, "There was no way he was going to help us. I shoulda known better." He kicked at a stone and sent it skittering across the car park. "This is worse than I thought. I suspect his indifference means there's somebody else involved, somebody flying cover for them. Highly placed. Up in the nosebleed section."

"Would you please stop talking like an American and repeat all that so I can understand?"

"Me doth protest, milady. I am an American." He turned to look at her face and was ambushed by her eyes, so intense, so caring. *Those eyes! Every time I look into them, I want to fall in headfirst.* He took a moment to collect his thoughts. "What I said is those guys last night weren't worried about getting caught. They're confident. Pretty bold talking in a pub. They probably have someone high in the police or the government to protect or cover for them. Deflect investigations. Discourage curiosity."

"Which government? Irish or Russian?"

"Hey, good point. Either. Both. But somebody's gotta be protecting them.

"I don't know who we can trust. Certainly not Hallums." Michael felt another wave of discouragement. "We need help. We have to talk to somebody. But why would anybody believe me?"

"Because, Michael, you are you. You are honest. You are so straight you make a ruler look like boomerang."

"Gee, thanks."

She held him by the shoulders. "Listen to me, Michael Anthony Callahan. You can't give up. We can't give up. We owe it to those girls who will be trafficked and forced to do terrible, horrible things if we quit." She wrapped her arms around him like the world would end if she let him go.

He buried his face in her hair. *Why can't life be more like the movies? In the movies, the good guys always know what to do. Life is simpler. Reality sucks sometimes.*

"What about the headmaster?" she whispered. "He would believe us."

"Probably. But when he went to the Garda, they would ask where he got the story, which would lead them back to us, the loony teenagers. So, nope."

"Okay, how about your authorities? Surely with your family connections, somebody in the embassy will listen. They can alert the Garda at a higher level than we can."

He thought that over. "I know where the American Embassy is, thanks to Séamus and my passport episode." He nodded. "Sure, why not? All I'm risking is a couple hours. And my life, holding onto you for the trip over there."

She lightly punched him on the arm and laughed. "You can ride the bus, boyo!"

CHAPTER THIRTY-EIGHT

U.S. Embassy,
Ballsbridge, Dublin

Ciara drove the scooter to the U.S. Embassy with urgency, weaving through the late afternoon traffic. Michael still thought the large building was a weird structure. He could see three stories of glass, though he knew from the Internet there were two more stories underground. The circular building was supposed to represent the early American flag, but he couldn't see any resemblance. To him, it looked more like a gigantic lumpy cheesecake covered with spangles. But Babushka, the artist, would love it.

Two lines of people waited to do business at the embassy, a short one for American citizens, the other for "All Others." Michael pulled Ciara into the citizen line with him and finally worked their way to the front gate, guarded by a U.S. Marine.

"Corporal, my name is Michael Callahan. I need to speak with the Air Attaché, please. Tell him that the grandson of Major General Sean Callahan, United States Air Force, needs to talk with him. It's important."

"The prisoner-of-war, Major General Callahan? The one who was rescued? The one in the book?" the now-awed Marine asked.

Michael stood as tall as he could. "He's my granddad."

"Wow. But I'll still need your passport, sir."

Michael handed it over. Ciara said, "I'm with him," and offered her identity card.

After a few minutes, another corporal appeared and gestured to follow him.

They were ushered into a lavish office. The brass nameplate on the walnut desk read "Colonel Neal Coyle, USAF." Colonel Coyle, a handsome, slender, mid-forties man with hair starting to go gray, looked like a recruiting poster for the Air Force with his tailored uniform and military bearing. He stood when they entered and extended his hand first to Ciara, then to Michael. "Neal Coyle. Glad to meet you."

Over Coyle's shoulder, Michael saw a wall covered with photos of Coyle in his flight suit standing next to a B-52 bomber, along with his commission and other mementoes of a distinguished career. Michael smiled to himself. His father and grandfather had the same kind of stuff on a wall in their offices, usually referred to in Air Force lingo as the "I Love Me" wall. Coyle motioned them into leather chairs.

"Colonel, thank you for seeing us. We wouldn't be here if it weren't important."

Coyle nodded. "The corporal said something about your grandfather being a major general?"

"Major General Sean Callahan, retired. My father is Colonel Thomas Patrick Callahan, also retired. Here's my military dependent card."

Coyle glanced down to read the information printed on the laminated card. "Your father is Tom Callahan?"

he said, surprised. "The Tom Callahan? The F-15 Eagle driver, Tom Callahan?"

"Yes, sir. That's him."

"I think I met your dad when I was in Panama for my first joint tour as a captain."

"Possible, sir. He was stationed in Bolivia and spent some time in Panama."

Coyle nodded, apparently satisfied. "What can I do for you?"

Michael gave the colonel a quick briefing on what they had discovered.

"Okay, Mike, my first question is: why don't you go to the Irish police?"

"Michael," said Ciara.

"What?"

"His name is Michael," she said again.

Annoyed, Coyle turned back to Michael. "Okay, Michael, why haven't you gone to the Irish police?"

"I tried, Colonel. Our local superintendent is not one of my legions of fans. He wouldn't listen. And if I jumped his chain-of-command, his superiors would think I was just another American lunatic teenager." He held out his hands, palms up, and shrugged.

Coyle sat back in his leather executive chair and thought for a moment. "You speak Russian?" he said, doubt in his voice.

"Sir, if you know my dad, you know that my grandfather was held prisoner in Russia for thirty years before my father could rescue him." He leaned forward in his chair. "Google it, sir. It's all over the Internet. There's even a novel based on the rescue. My grandfather home-schooled me in Russian. I speak it as well as I speak English."

"And Spanish and Italian," added Ciara, pride in her voice.

"Colonel, I—" Michael glanced at Ciara, embarrassed, then back to Coyle. "Sorry, I mean, Ciara and I don't know what to do next. The Irish authorities need to have this information. The Italians were eager to get the trafficking started."

Coyle dug out a yellow pad and produced a pen. "Okay, Michael, start over. I'll present this to the Legal Attaché." He glanced at his watch. "Tomorrow."

Outside the embassy, Michael said, "I'm not feeling this meeting either. He's going to slow-roll us."

"I agree. He didn't seem very concerned, like it's not an American problem."

"It's a human problem. It's also an American problem. The United States is the world's largest consumer of child slavery."

"Really? What happened to the idea of a good, clean-cut America?"

"Ciara, do you think there are creeps and perverts in smiley-face Ireland?"

"Of course there are."

"The population of Ireland is less than five million. The population of the United States is around 325 million. So if there is the same percentage of creeps in America as in Ireland, we should have roughly, what? Sixty-five times as many creeps running loose as in Ireland."

"Are those real numbers?" she asked, surprise on her face.

"The Internet hath spoken. Human trafficking is a massive stain on my country."

"You and your research Michael."

Michael looked down and shuffled his feet. *Why is this so difficult? What do we do now?* He thought for a moment, then turned back to Ciara. "My dyedushka has a saying that kept him alive in Russia—Never give up. Never, ever give up." He smiled. "Speaking of the Internet, I know someone we can use. Can you take me into the city?"

"Does the Pope live in Rome?"

Michael took Ciara's arm and aimed her toward the door. "Let's go. I'll tell you about it on the way."

CHAPTER THIRTY-NINE

Downtown Dublin

Michael and Ciara drove around the Trinity College area dodging cars and the crowds, searching for Internet cafés. Three seemed suitable, so Ciara parked her scooter and they wedged themselves into the pedestrian traffic. Michael checked out one café, then another. Too many people, too many ears. Café number three was nearly deserted. Michael paid for an hour of video conferencing in a glass booth. He made sure the door was secure and punched in Fabian's number while Ciara dug through her purse and produced a set of earbuds. She snuggled closer to Michael and slid her arm over his shoulders so they could share them.

Michael could smell her scent again. Simply dynamite.

Fabian answered on the first ring, his handsome face split into a wide grin. "Hey, amigo!" Michael sometimes felt he was looking into a mirror when he saw Fabian, even with the beat-up straw cowboy hat he always seemed to be wearing. Seated at the desk in his tiny bedroom, he looked as relaxed as Michael felt tense. Fabian did a double take as he noticed Ciara draped around Michael. "Whoa, who's this?"

Michael laughed. "Ciara, this is Fabian. Fabian, this is my friend, Ciara."

"Hello, Fabian. Michael talks about you a lot. Lovely to meet you."

"And you, Ciara."

Fabian switched to Tiwa. "So, Miguel, your Irish cultural search is going pretty good, huh, buddy?"

"Enough, Fabian," Michael said in English. "Dude, I need a solid."

"Anything *para mi hermano Boliviano*."

"Do a deep search of the Dark Net."

Surprised, Fabian said, "I thought we weren't going to do that anymore. Didn't we get in enough trouble last time? I almost got kicked out of school."

"This is different. This isn't casual exploration. This is serious stuff, man.

"I want you look for mentions of museum-quality Russian icons for sale. And any connection to the Hermitage Museum. Next, do oligarchs. No, first try *nomenclatura*, then oligarchs. They mean almost the same." He spelled it for Fabian.

"These the guys you told me were running Russia?" Fabian asked.

"Yeah. See if there is a connection between Russian icons being smuggled and oligarchs and Ireland."

"What's the big deal about smuggling icons?"

"I overheard some underworld types talking about smuggling stuff through Ireland. Italian Mafia and the Russian Red Mafiya joining together." Michael gave Fabian a quick summary of the events of the past twenty-four hours.

Fabian sat back in his chair, arms crossed. "I say again, what's the big deal about smuggling icons?"

"They also mentioned women. And girls."

"Wait, what?"

"Yeah. Exactly. Girls, dude."

"Whoa. They're smuggling girls? Human trafficking?"

"Not yet. But they're getting into the market, as they say."

Fabian settled back in his chair, deep in thought. "And why aren't you doing this Internet search, amigo?"

"I don't have the fiber connection you do, and I'm afraid somebody over here who's connected to these guys and playing computer defense might pick up my interest and track me down."

"Thanks a lot, bro."

Ciara spoke up. "Fabian, please help us. Michael tells me that you are quite the clever bloke."

Fabian seemed to melt at the sound of her voice. He grinned. "Well, since you put it that way, sure, why not?"

Michael laughed, certain that Ciara had just wrapped Fabian around one of her graceful pinkies. "There probably isn't anything buried so deep that you can't find it, Fabian, genius that you may be and all. While you're doing this, I think you're safe in Fortress America, especially hidden away on the Pueblo. But watch yourself, amigo."

"You know me. If there's something out there, I'll find it. But let me tell you, bro, this is dirty stuff. In Ireland of all places? Jeez."

"Yeah."

CHAPTER FORTY

INTERNET CAFÉ
DUBLIN
THE NEXT AFTERNOON

Michael and Ciara returned to the Internet café, which was library quiet and nearly empty, perfect for their purposes. Michael rented a booth, then placed a call to Fabian's voice mail to let him know they were in place and available.

While they waited for Fabian's call-back, Michael said, "I've been going over what the Italians said to the Russians in the pub. They made it clear that they expect top quality Eastern European girls and will pay accordingly. The Russians said okay, but it'll take some time to set things up. Apparently, there are new logistics requirements for live cargo as opposed to icons." He shook his head. "But the Italians demanded quick service. They were all talking about girls like they were nothing more than dining room furniture or something." He muttered under his breath.

"What was that last bit?" Ciara asked.

"Sorry." He felt his face grow hot. "It was a Russian curse."

"You said a curse word? You?"

"My grandfather spent thirty plus years in Russian gulags. He knows every filthy word in the Russian dictionary, plus a few that aren't."

"Your *grandfather* taught you to curse in Russian? Why ever would he do that?"

"I was getting in trouble in soccer games for yelling at bad calls. Now I do it in Russian and don't get yellow cards because the referees don't know what I'm saying. Believe me, I can swear like a Russian sailor on meth."

"Sounds like that could be fun!" Ciara winked.

"Well, one time I slipped up in front of my grandmother. She was horrified. When she discovered what my grandfather had taught me, she really let him have it, standing right next to me." He chuckled. "I learned a couple more words from her."

The computer screen came alive and Fabian appeared, dressed as usual like he just came in from breaking horses. "*Hola, amigos!*"

"Hey, Dude."

"Fabian, it's ever so nice to see you again."

Fabian smiled at Ciara, then shifted his attention to Michael. "I don't have much time right now, so let's get to it. I've been looking through the Internet as well as the Dark Net, *amiguito*. You're right about the icon smuggling. Stolen artwork is a massive market worldwide. Billions of dollars. I'm guessing that your Irish guys are specializing in Russian artwork."

"Yeah," Michael said. "Which means somehow the Hermitage Museum is involved. Looting the Hermitage is probably like mining gold for these guys. There isn't a single inventory document in existence. At least, that's the opinion in the art world that my grandmother lives in. Some of the items in the Hermitage collection were looted from Russian nobles after the Revolution. Possibly even some things taken from her relatives."

"Imagine that," Ciara sighed.

"I've been to the Hermitage with my babushka, Ciara. It's massive."

"He's been to Russia!" she said to Fabian, envy in her voice. "I haven't even left this island. Ever." She shook her head. "How ever did you learn all this about Russia and Russian culture?"

"My babushka is an artist. Art is a big deal in my family. We discuss art at dinner so I had to learn about art in order to eat. I know almost as much about it as I do about snowboarding. And Russia is another big dinner topic."

"I'm embarrassed that I don't know more about the country," she said.

"No worries. Most kids know next to nothing about Russia. Except maybe during the Olympics or the World Cup when they're in the news."

"Okay, people. We're getting off topic," Fabian said. "Another big question is why would Russians choose Ireland for a transit port?"

"Dublin is the biggest port in Ireland," Ciara added, "but it's not the biggest in Europe. Why here?"

"I'm guessing because there's a Russian community in Dublin to draw from," Michael said. "Maybe the guys here work part-time, meet shipments, then fade back into the Russian population. I bet my grandfather would say there has to be a big boss—and it's most likely a he because all the oligarchs are men. It'll be someone who can manipulate the Irish system and probably is reasonably sophisticated. Apparently, the plan is for the guys in Russia to use their network in Eastern Europe to supply the girls and arrange transport through their already existing icon smuggling pipeline to Ireland. Then they hand off the product to the Russian/Irish connection."

A couple students entered the café and started toward the booth next to theirs. Ciara waved to get their attention and pointed toward the booth down at the end of the row. They nodded and settled into a booth at the other side of the room.

Michael said, "My mom says businesses the world over have one thing in common—they all run on money. The bigger the company, the more money needed. Money to a company is like cocaine to an addict. Ya gotta have it. There is simply too much money in human trafficking; it's too profitable to be ignored. Women and children are expendable to those creeps."

"I did some net-crawling on human trafficking," Fabian said. "It's a growth business. Most of the articles say it's a pandemic actually. Demand is high. In the United States, human traffickers are often drug smugglers using their drug networks. And because of all the recent migrant flows, there is a pretty good supply of targets to choose from. Women and girls make up the bulk of the millions of present-day slaves, about seventy-five per cent, actually."

Ciara slammed her fist on the desk. "I'm sick of statistics! These are humans we're talking about, chaps, not numbers!"

"Shh! Keep your voice down," Michael warned, with a glance at the couple in the other booth. "Trafficking's much bigger than we thought, what most people think. Probably because it's illegal, people don't know how widespread it is."

"I don't need to hear any more, Michael. We have to do something. Everything we can."

Fabian joined in. "If we're going to catch them making a mistake, it's more likely to happen on the first couple shipments. They won't have a finished plan drawn up with the kinks worked out. Especially since this is a hurry-up job for the Italians."

"Where do we start?" Ciara asked.

"It's the network we're after," Michael said. "The guys here in Ireland and their peers in Russia are doing the stealing, the looting, the kidnapping. The oligarchs are doing the financing and using their business contacts and shipping lines make it all work while keeping their hands clean. But they're just thugs—low-class, well-dressed, greedy thugs. Up to and including the president. Russia is a kleptocracy. The rulers are stealing everything possible."

"Kleptocracy!" Ciara said. "Go on with you!"

Michael continued, "We have to go after the big fish. My mom, the economist, would say go for the money people."

"Wait! What? We're just teenagers," she said.

"Exactly. Nobody is taking us seriously. Which is why we need evidence, not just hunches. Proof. You and I will do what we can here. Fabian will troll the Dark Net."

"Then, we turn the evidence over to the police?"

"Then, we turn it over to the police or the embassy. The professionals, the adults. And we go back to being teenagers."

Ciara looked doubtful. "Promise?"

"Promise."

Fabian said, "Ciara, I gotta go *muy pronto*, but I need to say a few things to Miguel. In Tiwa. Okay with you?"

"Of course, Fabian. Thank you ever so much for all your help."

Fabian leaned as close to the screen as he could. "Dude, you need to be careful. This is way out of your league. You're just a kid. These guys are Mafia and Red Mafiya, weapons-grade bad asses and world-class murderers. They kill whomever, whenever, and wherever they want. The Russians are ex-KGB hoodlums. If you get in their way, they will kill you in ways you don't want to hear about. End of story. End of Miguel." He paused. "And your Ciara. Don't forget about her, *mi amiguito Boliviano*. Go to the cops! Find adults who will listen!"

"Fabian, there are no adults who will listen. And it's all about Ciara, too. I can't just leave. I can't leave her here alone to face down these creeps."

"Dude—"

"Don't dude me, bro. I've thought about this from every direction possible. It's my fault I got her into this. I have to get her—and the other kids who are gonna be shipped—out of it. If I bail out, people will die or get sold as slaves, which is worse. I am scared fartless. But I have to do something."

Fabian settled back into his chair. "Okay, man. We'll do it your way for the time being. We should always speak Tiwa, just in case, like the Codetalkers. And like your dad would say, keep checking your six o'clock."

"Always."

"*Adiós*, amigo."

"*Adiós*, Fabian."

The screen went blank.

Ciara asked, "What did he say to you?"

"Oh, just some stuff about being careful."

"He said my name," she said in an accusing voice.

"Of course he did. He thinks you're a total ten."

"A what?"

"A babe."

"Really?" Ciara smiled, crossed her arms, and settled back into her chair. "I rather like this Fabian chappie, don't I now?"

CHAPTER FORTY-ONE

Internet Café
Dublin

Michael checked the time on his phone. "Italy's an hour ahead. I'm going to call the guy I know in Rome."
"You mean your buddy, the Pope?" Ciara asked.
"What?"
"You know," she said with a grin. "The person Ms. Scher has you tweeting every week in Latin."
"No," Michael laughed. "Max Ewen, the guy I told you about from my flight over here. Lives in Rome. His mom works in the American Embassy. We've stayed in touch. I sent him an email this morning, so he's expecting me to call."
Michael pulled up Skype on the computer screen and punched in some numbers. Max's face appeared, and the boys waved as they greeted each other.
"Hey, Max! *E stato troppo tempo, amico mio.*"
"Hey, Michael. *Ciao, fratello!*"
"This is my friend, Ciara."
"Ciara," Max said with a smile.
"Lovely to meet you, Max."

"You look a lot better than the first time we met, amigo," Michael said.

"Thanks. I feel a lot better, too. Took up skateboarding because of you. Haven't injured myself yet."

"That means you're not trying hard enough." They laughed.

"Let me tell you the details I couldn't put in my email." Michael related what he heard in the pub plus what they had discussed with Fabian.

"You speak Russian?"

"*Da.*"

Max laughed. "You are full of surprises, *amico mio.*"

Ciara said, "That's what I say! No telling what this chappie is going to come up with next!"

"Off the top of my head," Max said. "All this sounds like something Russians would do. By the way, my mom says the Russian Mafiya makes the Italian Mafia look about as tough as a high school lacrosse team."

Ciara squeezed Michael's hand. "Just what I said to you."

Michael shrugged. "Any word about the Italian Mafia dealing in women?"

"Two things, Michael. First: Russia and Ukraine are the world's largest exporters of women. Fact. Second: The Italian Mafia has been dealing in women forever. Italy is awash in African immigrants—legal and illegal—so there's no shortage of people to snatch. I can see they'd like some Russian and Eastern European girls, especially blondes and redheads, to add to their product lines, so to speak. Sorry, Ciara."

"Yes, me, too, Max," Ciara said. "I'm sorry about the whole situation."

"All this makes sense to you?" Michael said.

"Oh yeah," Max said "Human trafficking is one of the big issues here in the embassy. My mom talks about it at dinner. We even talk about it in the international school. There are Russians all over Italy flashing wads of cash, buying big properties, fancy cars, yachts. Throwing big parties. All that dirty money comes from somewhere. There are few, if any, attempts at subtlety on the part of the oligarchs and their pals."

Silence. They stared at each other, each with their own thoughts.

Max broke the quiet. "Do you have any idea when the shipments are supposed to start?"

"Nope," Michael said. "Soon, though."

"Do you want me to speak to my mom about this? I can't tell you her position, but she's pretty plugged into the embassy here."

"Only talk with her to get information. Your mom doesn't know us. Heck, you and I only spent fifteen minutes together, so you don't really know me either."

"Listen, dude. Sorry to be that guy but somebody needs to remind you who you're dealing with."

Ciara poked Michael. "See!"

Michael said, "Yeah, I know. That's why we need to get some real info to the right people, then bow out. I got it. I got it!" He looked at Ciara, then back to Max. "Thanks for the offer of your mom's help but let's wait on that. Once we have proof, we might go to her."

"Okay, buddy. You did me a solid, and I owe you big time. But let me say that you need to be careful. And keep me in the loop. If I don't hear from you in a couple days, I'm going to my mom. For your protection, bro."

Ciara leaned toward the screen. "Deal, Max."

Surprised, Michael glanced at her, then back to the screen. "You heard her, Max. Forty-eight hours. If you

don't hear from either of us, talk to your mom." He added. "And I hope that she's as tough as mine."
"Oh yeah. Believe it, buddy!"

CHAPTER FORTY-TWO

The White Rabbit Pub
Eddington

Donal Gillmore watched as the pub gradually filled with the banter of arriving lunchtime patrons. He used to love the atmosphere and camaraderie of Irish pubs. Back in his previous life as an athlete, he spent many happy hours drinking with his rugby teammates after matches.

He was early for this meeting, as usual. He made it a point to show up early for his business appointments in order to choose the seats. He preferred to be in the rear of a pub where he could sit with his leg protected from careless patrons. It was also usually darker, which helped keep his two lives—as a history teacher and a smuggler—and two identities—Donal Gillmore and Dmitri Andropov—separate.

His companion for the afternoon was his old friend and former rugby teammate, Garda Superintendent Hallums. Gillmore knew that Hallums owed his position to his wife's political connections. He was not particularly bright, having made at least one too many tackles, but he was aggressive and persistent, useful traits for a police officer. Less positive, Hallums liked to jerk people around, make people wait for him, play power games. Gillmore tolerated Hallums' braggadocio because he provided the occasional useful bit of insider police information.

Hallums arrived fifteen minutes late. With a nod to Gillmore and no apology, he planted himself in the chair opposite and ordered his usual ploughman's lunch with a pint. The two men kept up a running commentary about the All Ireland Irish League rugby game between Hallums' favorite Cork Constitution and Gillmore's team, Dublin University, until the food arrived. Then, Hallums changed the subject.

"You wouldn't believe what one of your students told me," he said, mouth full of cheese and bread.

"Which one?"

"The pint-sized Yank." Hallums paused to gulp his beer. He shook his head as if still amazed. "The boy said he heard some Russian Mafiya types and a pair of Italians working out a deal to traffic girls through here. Most of the girls would be bound for Italy but the Russians wanted to cream off a few for the Irish market." He shook his head again. "The lad is daft."

Gillmore felt an icy cold wrap itself around him. *How could that possibly be?* He waited until he could ask with a smile and a normal voice. "Where did he get that information?"

"Said he overheard it while on a date with the Harrington girl at a pub. He claims he can speak Italian and Russian."

The night I was sick! I miss one meeting. One meeting, and those morons do this. He sipped his beer. "Does he now?"

"Dunno. He said some funny sounding sentences that could have been Russian or he could have been havin' me on. I don't speak the lingo meself. You know that."

"Can you remember any words that he used?"

Hallums paused for another gulp of beer and thought a moment. "A couple times he repeated something like *durak*. Do you know what that means?"

"A bit cheeky, that. If it's the same word that I know, it means idiot."

Hallums' face flushed, and he slammed his fist on the table. "That little—"

Gillmore had to bite the inside of his mouth to keep from laughing. *And he's right, Hallums, me boy. You are an idiot. But quite useful.* "Yes, quite. But no matter. I'll look into it."

"How?"

"Don't worry. We teachers have our methods."

CHAPTER FORTY-THREE

St. George's Teacher's Lounge
The next morning

Gillmore followed Ms. Scher into the lounge. "Good morning. I've been wanting to ask you about young Callahan. How's he doing in Latin?"
"Why do you care? I understand you threw him out of your class."
"Yes, and I feel bad about that."
"You should. He's an excellent student. A superior student, in fact."
"Yes, so I hear. I think I should perhaps make amends, don't you?"
She raised her eyebrows and cleared her throat. "Why Donal, that's, well, unexpected."
"No matter," he said. "I heard a rumor that Callahan was quite the linguist. Is that true?"
"I told you he is a superior student. He is simply ripping through Latin."
Gillmore nodded as if satisfied. "I understand he speaks Spanish. Does he speak anything else? Americans are not exactly known for their linguistic abilities."

"He speaks beautiful Italian. Learned on his grandmother's knee."

Gillmore nursed a secret anger for his parents for not teaching him Russian as a child. He understood why they didn't but still resented the fact that his Russian would always have an Irish flavor instead of a native accent. "Learning as a child isn't the same intellectual challenge as learning as a student. Not much credit there for Callahan's intellect. And Italian and Spanish are both Latin-based. No wonder he does well in Latin. Again, no real justification for calling him a superior student."

She stepped into his space and glared at him. "He also speaks fluent Russian!" she flared. "Having native-speaker fluency in four major languages by his age is a true accomplishment, Mr. Gillmore!"

So, it's true. I'll have to nip this right now before that brat finds someone who will believe him and ruins everything.

Gillmore grimaced in pain as he climbed the stairs into the student dorm area. He had chosen this time carefully because the building was off-limits to teachers, and he wanted to get in and out without being seen.

The hallway stretched out ahead of him. *How chert voz'mi will I find his room?* He noticed the nametags posted outside each door. *Very convenient.* He made his way down the hallway until he found Michael's room. After a quick glance up and down the corridor, he opened the door.

He was surprised by how neat the room appeared. He looked through the desk drawers, searching for something that concerned him. *There's the skateboard that I've heard so much about.* A fishing rod tube leaned against the wardrobe. There was a big box on the floor inside. Gillmore opened it. *A drone? Whatever does he have that for?* He didn't know anything about drones, but this one was obviously expensive. *Toys for the rich, I suppose.* He shook his head. *Bloody Americans.*

Satisfied, he slipped out the door and gently closed it behind him.

"Gillmore!"

He turned. "Headmaster."

"I'm surprised to see you. And why exactly are you in the dormitories, Mr. Gillmore?"

"I was looking for Callahan, Headmaster."

"Why?"

"I was a bit harsh on him, and I wanted to say that I regretted it. Smooth things over, you see."

"Teachers are not allowed up here. You know that. Find him in the school area for your apology."

"My error, Headmaster. It won't happen again."

"See that it doesn't."

Gillmore limped away. *You stupid git.*

As soon as Gillmore reached the school area, he stepped outside to use his cell phone. One of his pet Russians answered. "I'm glad you called, comrade," he said. "I reviewed the security tapes from a few days ago. There was a couple riding by on a scooter. They made several passes and seemed very interested in our building."

"Why are you mentioning this to me now?"

"I don't like it. It's suspicious."

"And?"

"I used one of our Garda contacts. The scooter is registered to a student at St. George's, a Ciara Harrington. Do you know her?"

Gillmore felt like he was punched in the gut. *This has to be stopped.* "Find the girl! You have her home address from the registration. She also works at the Lamb and Child Pub. You know it?"

"*Nyet*, but I can do a search and find it."

"Good. Stake it out. I planted a bug in the American's room." Gillmore thought some more. "Find the boy. He skateboards quite a lot after school. Find the parks and watch them. Learn his patterns. Now. Today."

CHAPTER FORTY-FOUR

Skateboard Park
Dublin

"Nate, can you take us to this location using the tunnels?" Michael held up a street map of Dublin and pointed to the city's old warehouse area.

"Dunno. Probably. But why?"

Ciara spoke up, "Let's just say that we're playing a hunch, Nathan me boy, and leave it at that."

"Go right now? I was planning on doin' some riding with you, Michael."

"It's important, Nate."

With a sigh, Nate took the map from Michael and studied it for a few moments. "I think so. We could sure try. We can take a bus from here to here," he pointed. "There's an opening around the corner near the Liffey, an old one I've only used once. We could get in there. It should save us some time."

"You'll do it?"

He nodded. "Sure. Why not? But first we need to get some things. It's likely to be wetter over there. We'll need some boots and torches. I'll round up some of the lads, and we'll be off."

"No, Nate. Just the three of us."

"Okay then," Nate said slowly. "I'll not intrude on your reasons now but we're going to have a talk when we're done."

They walked to the hideout where Nate rummaged in a second wardrobe and produced several pair of well-worn rubber boots. He motioned Ciara to a seat and slipped boots on her like she was Cinderella, which helped to break the tension. Michael put on his pair, stuffed some torches into his backpack, and they headed to the bus stop.

As they rode the bus through the city centre into the areas near the wharves, the streets became narrower and messier. A sense of dread filled Michael. All he knew was that he was getting deeper and deeper into a situation that he did not fully understand. He and Ciara were possibly the least likely couple in Ireland to take on serious Russian professionals. Yet here they were, trying another off-the-wall method of gathering evidence against the Russians. He glanced at Ciara. She looked almost bored. *What an actress she is. I know she's as frightened as I am. She's trying to keep Nate from guessing what we're up to. You go, girl!*

The bus crested a small hill, and the bay came into view in the distance. They made a point of being inconspicuous as they disembarked from the bus and headed toward the Liffey. Nate led them to the ragged edges of the river and started to cast about in the brush. "Here it is!" he shouted. They gathered around him and shifted some old boards that were in the way. Someone had cut through the iron bars that were supposed to keep people out. They slithered into the hole and pulled some of the boards back in over them.

This tunnel was as black inside as the ones they had explored closer to the skateboard park but had a less pleasant smell and was decidedly more humid. Water sloshed underfoot, just as Nate had predicted. The tunnels were narrow, walls covered with sheets of green slime from water dripping down the dirty brick surfaces. The ceilings were ragged with arches lower than before and not well maintained. They had to climb over several minor cave-ins as they made their way through the darkness, sidestepping trash as the tunnel snaked deeper into the old warehouse district.

The foundation indentations were farther apart, probably because the buildings above them were larger than those closer in the old city centre. One opened up into an overhead grate where Michael could get a location reading on his phone. He huddled with Ciara and studied the screen. "You were right," he whispered. "Some of these foundations drop into the tunnel. With any luck, maybe the Russians' warehouse does. Then, we might be able to access the warehouse through the floor or foundation."

"Or even just pop up nearby," she said. "That way we could get some proof."

They were close to their destination but not yet close enough. Michael gestured to Nate, and they continued into the darkness.

Suddenly, a rough wall of cemented blocks appeared in front of them. "This happens a lot," Nate said. "If I had thought to bring my tools, we could clear this away." He thumped the wall. One of the blocks fell with a thud on the far side. He shined his torch into the hole. "Some more of these blocks are loose. I can see down the tunnel. It keeps going a ways, but this is as far as we go today."

So close! Michael's shoulders slumped. *Will nothing ever go right for us?*

"I've seen worse, Michael," Nate said. "The tunnel goes on more. Maybe closer to your target, whatever that is. We're pretty close now, though." He turned and moved between Michael and Ciara. "Why are you so interested in this area? Why is this so important to ya?"

"Nate, it's probably better that you don't know."

"Hold on, pal. Something's up here." He stared down Michael. "What are you two doing?"

"You don't want to get involved."

"Michael, you're a good lad. And this Irish beauty is straight-up world-class. So, if you two are havin' to sneak around, something's wrong. You're my friends. It looks like you need some help. I want to help. So, open up."

Michael frowned, then looked at Ciara. She nodded.

"Okay, Nate," he said. "We'll tell you, and you can decide for yourself if you're in or not." He gave a quick summary of what they had learned and what they suspected.

Nate was silent for a few moments as he pondered Michael's words. "Why not just pass by the warehouse on your scooter again and get some photos? Or sneak in at night on foot?"

"This is not a neighborhood that kids normally drive around in. It's scary at night and taking pictures or looking in windows is too obvious in the day. By coming in this way, maybe we can get to the building through the tunnels, maybe not. Maybe we can get close enough to discover something that we can take to the Garda. We have to try something. I'm all out of ideas."

"What can I do to help?"

"Nate, this isn't just some street gang that we're up against. This is an international criminal corporation. Make sure you understand that. It will be dangerous."

Nate leaned against the wall, crossed his arms, and looked thoughtful. "Just thinkin' out loud, Michael. Me da doesn't have such a good relationship with the coppers. He had, shall we say, a troublesome youth. And is not popular with the Garda, even though he went straight when I was born. He's still a target of the Garda. We mustn't involve him."

"How about you? Are you involved now?"

"Wouldn't miss this for the world! Fightin' bad guys? It'll be like being on one of them shows on the telly!"

"Nate, this isn't some game, buddy. This is serious."

Nate put his hand on Michael's shoulder and looked him in the eyes. "I know, bro. But if we do this and catch the bad guys, we save some girls, give them their lives back." He paused and emotion crept into his speech. "And maybe, just maybe, we clear my family name with the coppers. Me da'll be able to live a better life, too."

CHAPTER FORTY-FIVE

St. George's College
Next morning

Ciara burst into the dining hall. Michael looked up from his breakfast and could tell at a glance that something was wrong. Way wrong. She rushed over and slid in across from him.

"Someone with a Russian accent called me mum. Warned her to make me stay away from the warehouse district! They must have seen me scooter last week and got the license number off the surveillance cameras."

"How would they track that down?"

"Police connections. They must have someone in the Garda working with them. Just like you said!"

They sat still, digesting this new development.

"I'm scared, Michael. They threatened my mother!" Tears leaked from her eyes, and she had a pleading look on her face. "I can't do this any longer. It's me mum, Michael, me mum! The stakes are too high!"

He took her face in his hands. She became perfectly still, her hands clutching his, her eyes cast down.

"I'm so sorry, Ciara," he whispered. "We're almost there. I promise we'll be more careful, get the proof, and end all this."

Ciara sobbed and shook her head. "It's too dangerous."

She wiped the tears away from her cheeks, pushed herself up from the table. "She says I have to stay away from you." More tears ran down her face. "I'm terrible sorry, Michael. Terrible sorry."

She turned toward the door and walked away without looking back. Michael watched her in shock until she disappeared through the doorway.

He knew she was right—her mother and brother depended on her. They were all she had, her entire family. He was just a boy who was leaving Ireland—and her—behind in a few weeks. This was the right thing for her to do. And the worst thing possible for him.

The pain of separation was like a hot spike driven into his gut, and his heart wrenched out of his chest. It was like nothing he had ever experienced. Just sitting in the dining hall was an ordeal. His world contracted around him. He was more isolated than ever before. Lonely, too, in the most profound sense, as lonely as he had ever been. He had camped by himself in the mountains, but that was being *alone*, not being lonely. He squeezed his eyes shut. There was a Ciara-shaped hole in his life where a romantic relationship should have been. The relationship had been so perfect—almost like in a fairy tale. The old fashioned kind that had perfect endings. What were the odds of this romance even happening?

Now it wasn't.

He fought the urge to run back to his room, lock the door, close the blinds, and hide in the dark. His hand shook as he took a sip from a mug of tea so stale he couldn't even revive it with three spoons of sugar. Despite his small circle of friends, life now wasn't—couldn't—be the same. Lonely didn't hurt like this. He searched for the best word: Devastated. Destroyed. Melancholy—that was the word. Melancholy, even worse than lonely.

His mind wandered. *Melancholicus as Ms. Scher would say. Грустный as Dyedushka would say. Melancolía as Fabian would say.*

No, he wouldn't. Michael shook his head in denial. *Fabian would never say the word melancolía—probably didn't even know it in Spanish. He would just say sad or gloomy or some other pithy word, then tell me to get off my ass and stop feeling sorry for myself.*

Why are you doing this fight against the traffickers, Michael me boy? he asked himself again. *It's dangerous, it's brutal, and it has the potential to grind you into little tiny pieces.*

All he knew was that he had to finish this. People's lives depended on it. The Callahans were all warriors. Even in Ireland, or maybe especially in Ireland, fighters were respected. Maybe his Bolivian ancestors were warriors. Maybe not. Maybe it wasn't in his blood, but it was certainly in his culture, his Callahan culture. He was determined to bring down these Russian *mudaki*.

He just wished it didn't hurt so much.

CHAPTER FORTY-SIX

Warehouse
Port of Dublin
Five o'clock a.m.

The office lights were set to low; Dimitri Andropov sat perfectly straight in his leather chair, hands folded on his desk. He half-opened one eye to check the time and groaned. His head pounded, and his sinuses felt ready to explode. Five o'clock Dublin time was eight in Moscow. The oligarch in charge of this first shipment of humans was an early bird. He had set the time for this call for his convenience, not Andropov's, who had dragged himself to his office on this cold, wet, rainy, and miserable morning, only to sit and wait.

He sighed as he settled back into his chair. Shostakovich's "Seventh Symphony" played softly in the background, and a cup of strong espresso sat on his desk. Andropov was alone in the cold warehouse. He routinely excluded his henchmen from listening to his confidential calls from Moscow as a security precaution.

This wait was longer than usual, which was not a good sign.

Andropov mentally arranged calls from Moscow into two main groups, one large, one small. The small group of calls was pleasant, appreciation for his work. The calls in the large group were harassing or threatening.

He suspected this call would be one from the large group.

He was correct.

Finally, the phone rang, and he shivered involuntarily. The voice on the phone was all business, not friendly. "We have almost enough for the shipment. Ten girls so far, all teenagers. Two more arriving here tonight. Are you ready? Is everything in place?"

"Da, comrade," he replied. "We have done what you ordered. We can accommodate all of them."

Andropov knew logistics, which was what smuggling was all about. True, handling live cargo did call for some adjustments, some different fittings in the container. Food, water, and air but nothing all that complicated. The girls would not be on a luxury cruise on the Queen Mary. They simply had to arrive alive and functioning. Let the Italians clean up any mess in Italy.

Then, the voice said, "I understand you have been sloppy."

"What?" Andropov blurted.

There was menace in the voice. "This program could have been compromised."

Andropov's mouth suddenly went dry, and his heartbeat rocketed up. "I don't know what you mean, comrade."

"Don't lie to me!" shouted the voice. "You were reported to the authorities by students, children!"

What? How would he know? How could he know? Thoughts tumbled in Andropov's head as he desperately tried to piece this together. Compromised? From his tame Russian lackeys? No, not possible. If they had reported the security breach, they would also be in trouble since they were the cause of this mess. It had to be someone else. Who then?

Hallums! It had to be Hallums. The man who related over a pub lunch what the Harrington girl and the American boy had told him—Russians were smuggling women for the Italians. Hallums must be a stooge for Moscow. How could he have not seen that?

This call was now a nightmare. It was clear that he had underestimated Harrington and the American, and overestimated Hallums. More threats spilled out of the phone. Andropov wanted to scream but knew better than to even raise his voice. There was only one person in the world who could shout down this particular oligarch and that was Russia's chief oligarch, the man who set up the present system. The Russian president.

Andropov clenched his jaw, said nothing, and absorbed the intimidation, the brutal words. He needed time to fix this.

The voice went silent.

"Da, comrade," Andropov said, a slight tremor in his voice. "I will correct the problem. We will get the product to market as planned. I would bet my life on it."

"You already have. Understand?"

"Understood."

The phone went dead.

Andropov slumped back in his chair and placed the phone on his desk with a shaky hand. His heart was racing, and perspiration beaded on his forehead. He knew he would only have one chance to prove himself to his Moscow masters. He was in their crosshairs. No mistakes would be tolerated.

He started laughing. A chuckle at first, then hysterical laughter. It was hilarious that he would not allow his

Russian minions to listen to his phone calls because he wasn't certain of their loyalty. Afraid they could betray him at any time. They were Russians, after all. He had been worried about them, and it was own friend, Hallums, the Garda superintendent who betrayed him, a man he had known since they were teenage rugby stars together. He took in several deep breaths and ordered himself to calm down. There was nothing funny about his present situation.

He promised himself that he would get even with Hallums, but right now, he had some more immediate business to deal with.

Those students ... clearly they had to be eliminated. Permanently. Andropov had experience eliminating troublesome problems. Callahan had to have an accident. No, better to have him disappear. Easier. Today.

As for this other problem ... he had the solution for that. Before shipping the captives to Italy, he would add one more young woman to make the shipment thirteen teenagers, a baker's dozen. Redheads were rare and prized in the Middle East. He would suggest to his Italian contacts that she be sold to an oil-rich sheik.

Perfect.

CHAPTER FORTY-SEVEN

St. George's College
Eight o'clock in the morning

Michael felt like he hadn't slept at all. He dragged himself into school. Latin class was a disaster. He wandered down the corridor toward the dining hall in search of a cup of tea, anything that could perk him up.

Hands grabbed at his arm.

Ciara!

She dragged him outside without a word, then turned to face him. "I talked with me mum. She told me she could take care of herself and for me to help you. 'Go to the Garda,' she said. I told her that we had. 'Then, go to the American Embassy,' she said. I told her we had done that as well. Then she said for us to do anything we can to help those girls."

Michael's mind was still spinning from Ciara's abrupt appearance. "She did? Really?"

"Yes!" she said. She moved closer. "*Yo te llamé pero tú no respondiste, mi amor.*" —I called you, but you didn't answer, my love. She ran her fingers along his jaw and across his cheek, then placed a gentle kiss on his lips.

Emotions swirled in Michael's body and his brain almost slammed to a halt.

Mi amor. She called me mi amor! She can't possibly understand how powerful that phrase is to a Spanish speaker.

Yes, she does! She's no dummy.

No, she probably saw it used in a movie or an adult book. She can't really mean it!

Yes, she does!

No, she doesn't!

"And you standin' there lookin' like a constipated greyhound."

"What?"

"Depressed, boyo. Down in the dumps. You look like you just lost your best friend."

He took her hand. "I did lose my best friend, but she's back now."

Ciara slid in closer. "Having said all that, boyo, what we have been doing is dangerous. Don't you think we should leave the smugglers alone?"

Michael looked at her for a long moment. His emotions churned, his stomach hurt. His hands were sweaty.

"I know, Ciara. I know it'll be dangerous. I know it'll be scary. That we can't trust anybody. I know that." He paused again. "When my family sits down to dinner, my folks often talk about subjects like ethics, developing a sense of justice, and ways to make the world a better place."

"Really?"

He nodded. "It's what parents do. Or at least, what my parents do. How can I ignore this situation when I know beyond any doubt that if my parents and grandparents were presented with a decision about walking away or doing the right thing, they would choose to do the right thing every single time, no matter how dangerous?"

"But they're super competent adults."

"Look around, Ciara. Next to our peers, we're at least competent, better than most even. But never mind the stats, we're it. It has to be us. There's no one else."

She smiled and slid her hands up his back. "I knew you'd say that."

"What? Was that some kind of character test?"

"Top marks, me darlin' boy. Top marks." She smiled again. "I just needed to hear it again—to bolster my confidence."

"Babe, I couldn't do this without you. Not a chance." He wrapped his arms around her and hugged as hard as he dared.

She kissed him again and again, like lightning would strike her if she stopped.

Seriously, this was one of the best things ever. Certainly worth being late to class.

"You are a gentleman," she whispered. "Not in a chauvinistic way but because you're a nice person. A caring person. A strong person. A gentle man."

Yeah, a gentle man who is about to get us killed if he doesn't think of something. And quick.

CHAPTER FORTY-EIGHT

SKATEBOARD PARK,
DUBLIN
LATER THAT AFTERNOON

What's taking him so long? Michael sat under a shelter and watched as the rain pelted down. Despite wearing a rain jacket, he was soaked from the knees down like he had waded through an acequia ditch without wearing his boots. Raindrops pounded the sidewalks and sluiced down the road. Impatient, he glanced at his phone. *Nate was supposed to be here fifteen minutes ago.*

All of a sudden, there he was, glistening in the rain, wearing a backpack and a grin. He carried two short handled shovels, and the backpack bulged with more tools. "We may have to do some digging. Might as well be ready for it. We'll knock some bricks away and make openings where we need them. Easy peasy."

"Thanks for meeting me," Michael said. "This has to be done super quick. Those girls could be loading right now."

As they rode the bus, Michael showed Nate a new GPS locator he had purchased along with the best Dublin street map he could find. "I marked the warehouse and loaded the coordinates in the GPS to help us know when we're close."

Great sheets of rain, thick, dark, and heavy made the search for the tunnel opening a cold, wet, and miserable experience. It was almost a pleasure to slide into the hole just to escape the weather. Michael was still surprised about how comfortable he felt underground. It was just as dark and difficult to slosh through the tunnel as before, yet now it almost felt normal. *Maybe it's because I have a destination in mind. Or maybe that the end is near. Either we find a way to get into the warehouse, or we don't. If this doesn't work, I'm going to have to get Dad to call the Ambassador. Or send a rocket up Colonel Coyle's butt. Or both.*

They made short work of the wall that had stopped them the previous day. Nate hacked at the stone blocks; Michael pulled them out of the way. They clambered through the hole and continued down the dark tunnel past several openings. This was all new territory to both of them. Nate had no idea of the structures above and they had to climb out into the rain twice to get their bearings and a GPS reading before they came to another obstruction.

Nate hammered away for a few minutes and climbed up the jumbled stones to shine his torch into a small opening. "This is no normal wall," he said. "This is a cave in. We'll not be able to get through, my friend."

They backtracked about fifty yards to the last opening, which put them right on the River Liffey. "This is it," Michael said. "I'll have to get out and see what I can see."

It took them nearly twenty minutes of sweaty work to make the opening large enough for Michael to squeeze through, and then he had to swing himself up a steep slope, wet and slippery.

The rain pounded down making the cold late afternoon air even colder. Thick clouds passed by overhead reflecting the ground lights. But they were closer than he had thought.

He leaned down the slope and said, "It's still raining. Maybe it will help me. You stay here. I'll be back as soon as I can."

Nate stuck his head out of the opening and looked up at Michael. "I'm not staying behind like your pet horse, Mr. Wild West American."

"You need to stay here in case something happens to me, Nate. If I don't come back, you go get Ciara and find somebody who will listen. Maybe a missing American student will get their attention."

Nate stopped his efforts to climb out and relaxed, as if considering the words. He nodded, reluctance written on his dirty face. "I don't like it, but you're right, you bloody Yank."

Michael pulled out his map, located his position, and tried to memorize the shortest route to the warehouse. Only a few blocks. "Thirty minutes."

He made his way down the gritty, deserted streets, sliding from one dark area to another, avoiding potholes and trash. He was surrounded by dirty buildings and ugly warehouses, a blighted area that apparently the Dublin public works department did not know existed. This was not a pedestrian friendly zone. No coffee shops or pubs. Few lights. Not his kind of place.

Michael found himself skulking in a narrow alley, wet to the skin, and totally clueless about what he was doing. Mental images of girls locked in containers gave him the strength to keep moving.

He paused before the last corner and leaned against a building to get his pounding heart under control. He heard an engine and tires on wet pavement. Michael froze and held his breath, listening for more. The vehicle sounds faded, though he couldn't be sure if it was just wishful thinking. He waited until he was dizzy before he drew another breath. Now he heard nothing. He lowered himself onto his belly and inched forward to peek around the corner.

He knew there had to be security devices like cameras and alarms. Russians were paranoid about security. The warehouse was probably more protected than Fort Knox. He couldn't possibly break in undetected. Where was an opportunity? What exactly was he looking for? Maybe this wasn't the best idea he'd ever had.

He glanced up. *There are the clear second story windows, just like I remembered. Dirty but not painted over. Looks like there may be a couple skylights. That's a surprise, considering that the warehouse looks like it hasn't had any maintenance in decades.*

Ah, I know how to do this!

He crawled backward away from the corner, stood, and moved as nonchalantly as he could back toward the river. He forced himself to maintain a normal pace and kept close to the walls and through as many dark areas as he could find. At the river, he oh, so carefully let himself down the slope. Only when Nate grabbed his legs and pulled him safely inside the tunnel could he relax.

He sat down, pulled his water bottle from his pack, leaned against the wall, and took a healthy swig. "Am I ever glad to see you, pal!"

"And?" asked an irritated Nate. "What's the deal?"

"Tonight, I'll get my drone up there and peep in the windows."

"A drone? That's your answer?"

"Maybe we'll get lucky and find a skylight. Most people don't think in three dimensions, so they didn't cover the windows up high. Maybe they're exposed to aerial surveillance. I can fly it from the street. I'll come back late tonight and hide in one of the doorways across from the warehouse. Even if they see me, I can run back here and escape using the tunnel."

"You can fly a drone at night?"

"Yeah … well, actually I never have, but I don't need to do anything fancy. It'll be a bit tricky, but I sure can't stand out in the street during the day and fly it."

"I still don't get it. These guys are in a warehouse, dummy. How can you get anything useful from a drone?"

"Video, dude, video! Maybe I can tilt the camera down into the warehouse through a window or a skylight and catch them doing something illegal, see some contraband, or something. How do I know what's in there? But maybe something will show up, something tangible to make our case with the authorities. Maybe that will get things moving."

Nate was clearly not convinced. "That's a lot of maybes."

"Do you have a better idea? I don't know what else to do."

"I knew I shoulda gone with you," Nate muttered. "Okay, *assuming* you're right and *assuming* we don't get caught, what do we do with the video?"

"Ciara checked out Interpol, the European police. It has a Human Trafficking and Drugs section. Send it there."

"Trust her to find that out. Sounds like a good place to start. Do an end around the Garda." Nate paused. "Okay. But tonight we turn the video over to the cops. Or Interpol. Or some organization that's full of adult professional-type people. Tonight. We are seriously over our heads here, bucko."

"You bet. Get back here, get the drone up, get some pictures. Download them and email to Fabian, then to Colonel Coyle at the Embassy."

"And Interpol," Nate added.

"And Interpol." Michael clapped Nate on the shoulder. "We could have this wrapped up by lunch tomorrow. Back to being kids again."

"I'll be with you tonight."

"No reason for you to get involved again, Nate. It'll be dangerous."

Nate pointed down the tunnel. "I don't see any bread crumbs behind you, my friend."

"What?"

"How do you think you'll find your way back here by yourself? You didn't leave any markings, a trail of breadcrumbs like in the fairy tales. You'll get so lost in those dark, dark tunnels you might end up in France. You call me, set a time, and I'll meet you at the skateboard park."

Michael thought his words over, examined them from as many angles as his tired mind could come up with. Nate made sense. And frankly, he was reassured by Nate's calm presence. "Okay. Let's meet at seven."

Nate made an exaggerated bow. "I shall clear my social calendar for you, my lord." He grinned, "Will ya be bringing Ciara?"

"Don't know. She hasn't told me yet what I want."

Nate laughed. "Whatever she decides to do, she'll do. And so will you."

"No kidding."

CHAPTER FORTY-NINE

DUBLIN

Michael was in a strange, almost euphoric mood as he left Nate behind at the park and made his way down the street to catch a bus to meet Ciara. Actually, he admitted to himself, he was more anxious to see her again than to give her a briefing on his new plans. This was turning into a pretty good day, especially after such a soul-crushing start.

He whistled as he eased his way down the tree-lined street, mentally scanning through his plans. The rain had stopped and the humidity, mixed with the delicious smells drifting out of multiple pubs, made him remember that he had missed lunch. The sidewalks were crowded with shoppers, ordinary people doing ordinary things. The clouds were thinning out enough to promise a sweet sunset. A block ahead, he saw the stone arch over the entrance to one of Dublin's massive parks, this one surrounded by an impressive eight-foot-high Georgian-style red brick wall.

He had begun the afternoon with the ever-helpful Nate for one more look at the warehouse, casing it, as they would say in a television detective show. With the drone, he now had a chance to get some physical visual proof the Russians had a human trafficking operation going full bore right here in Ireland's capital. If so, he would give that evidence to the authorities.

All he wanted was to get back to being just an anonymous and insignificant exchange student so he could concentrate his attention on the amazing Ciara and she on him. That would be heaven-like after all the pressure they both had been under. Things were finally looking up, and there was a light at the end of a very long and scary tunnel. Maybe his optimism was a result of his legit DNA kicking in, generations of fighting for life in the Bolivian mountains. Maybe it was his Callahan culture, generations of struggling for survival in the harsh wetlands of Ireland. Maybe both. He grinned. *Hey, maybe I'm not such a bad cultural combination after all.*

The waiting was the hard part. Michael considered himself somebody who got things done. Now. Right away. Patience was way down the list of his personal traits. He mulled over some potential options. He knew his next two moves, but what about after that?

He heard Ciara's voice in his head, *Slow down, Michael, me boy. You're gettin' ahead of yourself, aren't you now?* He laughed. She was everywhere, even in his mind.

A black panel van roared out of the traffic and screeched to a halt next to him. Two enormous men, dressed in black and wearing black ski masks leaped out and ran straight at him.

Russians! They must be Russians!

He bolted. One Russian grabbed for him and almost punched Michael down. Michael staggered, regained his balance and momentum, and ran into the street. A car screeched to a halt, burning rubber. He dove at the car, planted his hands on the hood, and flipped over. He landed on his feet and sprinted for the park.

In front of him were acres of space, wide open and deadly. The Russians were like NFL-quality athletes, huge and fast and right behind him. He had no chance in a foot race with these monsters. He could hear their breathing and their curses as they closed in.

He scanned left. Nothing but more open land. His eyes searched for obstacles that he could hurdle or leap or dive over. The Russians would have to climb or go around. To his right, lots of steps and concrete pathways. Perfect! He zigged left. The Russians altered course to cut him off. He zagged right to head into the cluster of brick paths, ramps, and buildings. He took each feature one at a time, the bigger the better. He vaulted a metal-pipe fence. Sprinted toward a series of low concrete walls. He planted a foot on a boulder and leaped to the top of a brick wall, then over, stuck the landing, and dashed away.

His body was in full fight-or-flight mode, heart pumping, adrenaline surging, lungs screaming. As athletic as the Russians were, his only hope was his quickness and parkour training. He ran, vaulted, dove, and rolled for his life.

A wall. He needed a wall, his specialty. There! Thirty yards away. A ten-footer surrounding some low buildings. He aimed right at it. He felt the Russians closing in again, then he was up. He pulled himself up onto a roof, just out of their grasp. He sprinted down the length of the building, leaped across a gap onto the roof of the last building. Down the length of that structure. An eight-foot gap to the perimeter brick wall. He looked behind him. No Russians. He turned toward the wall, did a balance jump, teetered slightly on the ledge, then dropped to the ground with a half-twist.

He stuck the landing and took a quick breath. The outside world was not yet a safe place. He couldn't see the

Russians, but he knew they would find him if he stayed where he was. Michael was gassed after all that running. His adrenaline meter was red-lined and his heart felt like it was about to burst.

No time to rest. He forced himself on and ran down the main street away from the black van to the nearby taxi stand and dove into the first vehicle. He slammed the door after himself and almost shouted the address of St. George's College.

Gotta warn Ciara!

CHAPTER FIFTY

TAXICAB
DUBLIN

In the cab, Michael tried to control his pounding heart rate. His stomach twisted, and he was burning up. Sweat matted his thick hair and ran into his eyes. His mind raced as fast as his pulse. *Think, Michael, think!*

He pulled out his phone, which had miraculously not been lost in the park, and called Ciara's phone. No answer. He left a voicemail for her to call him immediately. Five minutes later, he tried again. No answer.

His phone rang. *Ciara!* He fumbled for it. "OMG, I'm so glad you called! Where are you?"

Silence.

Then, a deep voice speaking Russian. "We have the girl. We will kill her unless you do exactly as we say."

Oh no! Think! … Stall them! … He sat, frozen in place. He had to maintain control. Ciara's life depended on it. He clenched his jaws, squeezed his eyes together, and pounded his fist on his leg.

"I don't believe you. Prove it. Let me hear her."

A few agonizing seconds of silence, then Ciara shouting, "Let go of me, you bloody wanker! Michael, don't listen." He heard sounds of a struggle and Ciara screamed. "Don't come here. They'll kill you!" The phone went dead.

Moments later, the phone rang again. He took a breath, then answered. It was the deep Russian voice again. "Come here, *Amerikanets*. Alone. No tricks, or she dies." The voice recited an address, then clicked off.

Michael dropped his phone into his lap and covered his face.

"Are you all right, mate?" asked the taxi driver. It was pretty obvious he wasn't.

"Yes, yes. Please, can't you go any faster?" He mentally raced through his options. *Fabian! I need to speak to Fabian.* He sent a text. *Amigo, get to your computer ASAP! Emergency!*

CHAPTER FIFTY-ONE

St. George's College

Michael crashed through the door to the dorm, slamming it against its stop. He took the stairs two at a time, ran into his room, slammed his door shut, and grabbed his laptop. "Hurry computer, boot up, boot up! What a mess!"

After what seemed an eternity, his screen lit up. He punched the keys needed to connect with Fabian.

Fabian's face appeared, full of concern.

"Fabian! Dude, call my dad … now! Tell him about the Russian Mafiya here in Dublin, the human trafficking stuff."

"Bro, what's goin' on? Wait. Let's go full *Tiwa*. Remember?"

Of course! Michael, you dummy! He switched to *Tiwa*. "Tell my dad what we've discovered, that the local cops won't listen to me and that I went to the embassy to see the Air Attaché. Remember his name?"

"Coyle?"

"Yeah. Colonel Neal Coyle. He knows my dad. Tell Dad that Coyle thought I was just some nut case kid." He rattled off Coyle's office phone number. "Have my dad call Coyle and chew his ass—he knows how to do that."

"Oh yeah. I've heard him once or twice."

"And get Coyle to call the Garda or whoever else he thinks is the best ... then get Dad calling people, starting with the White House."

"It would be better for you to call, Miguel. Save time."

"I don't have time! Listen to me, Fabian! The Russians have Ciara!"

"Jesucristo! What?"

"And they want me!"

"What do you mean, they want you?"

"They called me with her phone. One of the Russians told me to meet them at their warehouse. Or else." He scrunched his eyes shut as he recalled her terrified voice. "Or else they'll kill her."

"Miguel, *amigo mio*, go to the cops," pleaded Fabian. "They'll believe you now that the Russians have Ciara."

"No time! I have to go. Maybe the Russians will let her go if they have me."

"Don't go, *'mano*. That's the way it always works in the movies. They'll lure you in and kill you and Ciara and everybody else. Don't be a hero, dude."

"I'm no hero. But it's all my fault. I screwed this up so bad I can't let anything happen to her. I have to go try to fix this, Fabian. I'll think of something. If I had done this right, nobody would be getting hurt."

The brutal truth was that he had set Ciara up, marked her for retaliation from the Russians. But now, at least, he had something concrete he could do to atone for his errors.

Come on, get moving, Michael. Ciara's life depends on it. "Tell my father he's my only hope. Adios, amigo."

He tore through the dorm hallway, down the steps, and out on the college driveway toward the main street, heart pounding, lungs burning, rain coursing down his face and eyes, desperate to find another taxi.

CHAPTER FIFTY-TWO

A̧ndropov's Office
Warehouse, Dublin

Andropov leaned over his desk computer, an exquisite antique teacup in hand, and adjusted an external speaker. Next to him stood Ciara, hands tied, flanked by his two thugs holding her by the arms.

They could hear Michael as he crashed into his room, agitated, talking to himself. "Hurry, computer, boot up, boot up! What a mess!"

Andropov turned to Ciara, "I bugged his room for just such an occasion," pride evident in his voice.

Michael's voice came through clearly. "Fabian! Dude, call my dad…now! Tell him about the Russian Mafiya here in Dublin, the human trafficking stuff."

"Bro, what's goin' on? Wait. Let's go full *Tiwa*. Remember?"

Unintelligible words poured from the speaker, agitated but meaningless to Andropov.

"What?" he bellowed, staggering to his feet and wincing as pain lanced through his bad leg. "What's he saying?"

Ciara laughed, "My Michael's smarter than you. What a surprise."

Andropov listened, helpless, then hurled his cup against the wall. Shattered pieces of the priceless cup flew about the room.

Ciara laughed again. He slapped her hard. She let loose with a string of Irish oaths.

Regaining his composure, Andropov said, "Hardly an appropriate vocabulary for a lady, my dear Harrington."

She looked up at him, dripping blood from her nose. "It's exactly appropriate for a lady who has been kidnapped by mobsters and beaten, you disgusting human. How could you stoop so low?"

He grabbed a handful of her hair and yanked her upright. She stood on tip toes and writhed in pain. His face contorted with rage and he screamed, "What is he saying? I know he's talking about my plans. Tell me or so help me …!" He tightened his grip on her hair and twisted his wrist.

Ciara laughed through her agony. "He's speaking a Native American language. Even if I could understand my Michael, I wouldn't tell you a word."

"Your Michael indeed." Andropov released her hair. "He and his family are all filthy capitalist pigs, living off the sweat of workers. He doesn't care for you. He and his kind use the rest of us."

"Yeah? You and your politics. And here you are selling girls into lives of prostitution and disease and early deaths! Some humanitarian!" She cursed him again in Irish.

"Tie her to that chair," Andropov ordered. "And shut her up." He slumped back into his leather chair. "Then, go outside and intercept her boyfriend; make sure he's not followed."

CHAPTER FIFTY-THREE

Port of Dublin

The Russians caught Michael six blocks from the warehouse.
There were two of them, maybe more. He wasn't sure because they hit him so hard he blacked out. When he came to, he was hooded, tied, and dragged out to a car. They slammed him into the trunk and sped away.

He was trussed like a turkey, arms pinned behind his back, feet together. His head pounded. He felt the car making multiple turns on the pot-holed warehouse area streets. He bounced and rolled about in the foul-smelling trunk, thumping into hard metal. The tire jack stabbed him in the back.

Even woozy from the beating, Michael knew he was in desperate trouble. The men who held him were Russians and Russians made their own rules.

The car stopped. He heard the grind of an electric motor outside. *The garage door!* He must be at the warehouse.

The Russians carried him through the building like he was no more than a rag doll. They dumped him on the floor, and someone yanked off the hood.

Michael's fingers were numb from the plastic ties around his wrists. His body was on fire with pain. He opened his eyes just long enough to get a snapshot of the cavernous room before being blinded by the light. When he looked again, he saw Ciara strapped in a chair against the wall, gagged and bound, eyes wide with fright. His spirits soared. *Thank God, she's still alive!* He gave a slight nod, then winked. Painfully, he swiveled his head to look up at his chief captor.

And there, behind a massive stone table, sat Mr. Gillmore, granite-calm, a Russian Mafiya don. A gangster camouflaged as a high school history teacher. *Of course. It had to be him. I shoulda known.*

Michael struggled to sit up, causing the Russians to laugh at his helplessness. He turned sideways and awkwardly gestured with his bound hands. "What, you're afraid of me, Gillmore? Have to keep me tied up? Me? All 135 pounds of me? Man, you are a wimp. World-class, pal."

Enraged, Gillmore gestured to his henchmen. "Cut him loose."

One of the Russians produced a knife and slashed the plastic ties around his wrists and legs.

Michael struggled to his feet, rubbed his wrists to get the circulation going again. He locked eyes with Gillmore. "And Ciara, if you please."

His captor did not respond. "It is not my intention to please, Callahan."

"Oh, get serious. What do you have to be afraid of?"

Gillmore sat a moment, as if considering the challenge. Finally, he motioned to the larger thug to release Ciara. She tried to stand but the thug shoved her back into the chair.

Gillmore slowly got to his feet. Leaning heavily on his cane, he hobbled around the table right up to Michael. "I'm actually glad to see you here, Callahan."

"Not bloody likely, Gillmore!"

"In this building, my name is Andropov," he said in Russian.

Michael stared into those cold, slate-gray eyes and reminded himself that the real Andropov had been the head of the KGB, known for his brutality. He knew the night was about to become dirty, downright ugly.

"Call you Andropov? You've gotta be kidding," Michael said in the same language. "You're not a Russian any more than I am. You're a Russian wanna-be, Gillmore. Even your Russian is laughable—wouldn't earn a C grade in any decent language program."

Gillmore swung a savage backhand that smashed squarely on Michael's left cheek and knocked him down to the carpeted floor. Michael tasted blood. His face hurt, his arms hurt, his ribs were bruised and screaming. He struggled to stand, but one of the thugs knocked him down again. Despite the agony, Michael rolled onto his stomach. He raised himself up on his hands and knees and was rewarded with a swift kick to his side. He crashed back down.

Ciara screamed, "Michael, stay down! Please, me darlin' boy!"

Michael shook his head trying to clear the fog. Pain shot through him, and he felt the blood pulse in his battered face. He forced himself to stand. As he swayed, blood dripped from his broken nose into his mouth. He spat some out onto the carpet and locked eyes with Gillmore. He stood as tall as he could and pretended he was brave.

Michael dredged up every Russian curse word he knew and launched into a halting, defiant speech.

Gillmore spoke, again in Russian, "Mikhail, I'm impressed by your vocabulary. You are quite a young man. It's a pity that you chose the wrong side."

Michael said nothing.

"When were you alerted to our, ah, little enterprise here?"

Michael debated whether to lie but decided the truth would be better. "I heard your thugs talking with the Italians about smuggling. I know what icons are." He decided to keep the details to himself to protect Ciara.

Gillmore seemed amused. "It appears that there is more to you than meets the eye."

"I get that a lot. Just because I'm small doesn't mean that I don't have my talents."

Gillmore lifted one eyebrow. "Agreed. Clearly, that is a mistake I shall not make again, Mr. Small-But-Talented Callahan." He smoothed what remained of his hair and lapsed into a thoughtful silence. "You are not nearly as clever as you think, young man," he said and turned away, leaning heavily on his cane. It was a deliberate display of disrespect.

Gotta keep him talking. Maybe he'll let Ciara go. Michael switched to English. "How did you create this scheme of yours, Mr. Mastermind?"

Gillmore stopped, turned around, and leaned on his cane. "My parents were sent here by the KGB to infiltrate Irish society, undercover to be ready. During *The Troubles*, my parents helped with the rebellion, smuggling in guns, explosives, and money. I was born here."

He paused, as if considering how much to say, then continued. "When I was a teenager, my parents were killed in a car crash on the way to one of my rugby games. Probably murdered by your CIA. I had to re-invent myself, so I attended university in Dublin with help from friends of my Russian family. Opportunities appeared when needed as I progressed into society." He stopped and looked to Michael and Ciara as if expecting applause.

"You're a legend," Michael said.

Gillmore positively preened. "I'll take that as a compliment."

"No, dummy. According to my dad, a legend is the CIA term for a spy like you, undercover so deep that you can't be discovered. A created life, papers, career, few personal details. As ordinary as possible." Michael paused and said, "As *ordinary* as possible." He shook his head. "You had all the help the KGB and the oligarchs could give you, and yet somehow, a kid, a *kid*, discovered your filthy little enterprise. You are not particularly good at anything, Gillmore. You're as bad a spy as you are a history teacher."

A flush spread across Gillmore's face, and his eyes narrowed. "You don't know enough to play on this stage, Callahan."

"Hey, I'm only sixteen, I'm not supposed to know anything. For example, I don't know why you would do this, smuggle children, human slaves here in the twenty-first century. What kind of monster are you, anyway?"

"You are such a child."

"Yeah, well, you're not as smart as you think you are, Gillmore. This *child* caught you, didn't I?"

"What about your little friend, Callahan? Don't take all the credit."

"She knows nothing. You said that you would let her go if I came. Well, here I am. Let her go."

Gillmore laughed. "Let her go? Hardly. My, my, such an innocent. So naïve."

"Congratulations, slime ball. You've managed to capture and beat up a couple teenagers. What a victory."

Michael choked out a laugh—it really hurt. "But now you're gonna have to deal with my father, who is neither a child nor naïve … and, in fact, is quite good at neutralizing bad guys. He's coming and he's coming after you. He will track you down if it takes him a decade, no matter what rock you hide under. You won't escape."

"Your daddy? Oh, I'm terrified." Gillmore and his Russian thugs laughed.

"You should be. My dad outsmarted the entire Russian government to rescue my grandfather. Read the book, smart guy. It's easy to find. He's an advisor to the President of the United States. Well, maybe not officially anymore, but he used to work in the White House and has been friends with every American president since he left Washington." Michael paused to take a breath. The pain from his cracked ribs forced him to bend over. He made himself stand straight.

"More importantly, my dad knows the Russian president. You won't even be able to hide in Russia. Not after being publicly linked to kidnapping and prostituting adolescent girls. Even the Russian president won't protect you. You screwed up. You are radioactive, dude. Your oligarchs will flee like the cockroaches they are. They'll disavow any knowledge of you, just like they do in the movies. You are as good as fried, pal."

Ciara jumped up from her chair. One of the Russians grabbed at her, but she was too quick for him. She ran over and stood beside Michael. Her hand found his and he immediately, crazily, felt better. The situation was still critical and he knew in his heart he would not survive, but somehow, it was better now.

Ciara said in a soft voice, *"Casi lo hicimos, mi amor ¿no?"*—We almost did it, my love, didn't we?

His grandfather's words echoed in his brain, the words Dyedushka had used to survive thirty years in Russian captivity. *Never give up. Never, ever give up!*

Michael looked around, taking in the room, Gillmore, and his two thugs. He lowered his head in apparent defeat while he gauged the distance to Gillmore.

He spoke to Ciara in a low voice using simple Spanish. "*Mi amor*, you need to get away. Do not argue for once. Save yourself. Use the tunnel. Get to the authorities." He paused. "*Vaya con Dios, mi amor.*"

He took a deep breath. "When I say run, you run." He gave her hand a squeeze. "*Lista? Uno, dos, tres, Corre! Corre!*"

Ciara bolted between the Russians straight at the door. Michael took two steps, then dove into Gillmore. He smashed into him as hard as he could, directly on Gillmore's knee. The old guy screamed and crumpled, grabbing at his leg.

The Russian bodyguards lunged for Michael. He managed to kick one in the groin. The other one tackled him and pinned him down. Michael convulsed as agony shot through his body.

Ciara!

CHAPTER FIFTY-FOUR

St Anthony's Hospital
Dublin

Michael woke up, gradually swimming out of a vortex of pain. His headache was catastrophic, and he could barely move. "Where am I?" he croaked.

"Shh, Michael, me darlin' boy. Rest now. Go back to sleep. I'll be here."

He slipped back into darkness into another dream. Pain seeped away, and he floated. He saw green hills surrounded by high, snow-covered mountains and dotted with animals. Strange animals he recognized now. Dark-haired people who looked like him, smiling and speaking words in another language that made sense. Soft guitars fused with panpipes played beautiful melodies. He felt at ease, contented.

He slowly woke up again and peeked out of half-closed eyes, irrationally hoping that if he didn't open them all the way, he wouldn't feel all the pain. Wrong. He was in a bed in a room with white walls. He saw a tube attached to his right arm, and almost every part of his body that he could see was wrapped in bandages. His pain index was off the charts. He didn't want to move. The only thing that didn't hurt was his hair.

Ciara leaned over him, her long hair brushing his face. "Whoa, Ciara," he murmured. "Nice shiners!"

"Ha!" she said with a giggle. "You should see your face, boyo." She gave him a soft kiss. "Welcome back to the world, me darlin' boy. You've been down for almost forty-eight hours."

He tried to move his head to look around the room, and pain ripped through his neck and shoulders. "Where am I? What happened?"

"Shh, Michael. Lie back and close your eyes. Rest is what you be needin'."

"No, please raise my bed so I can see you."

"Even with my black eyes?" she teased. She found the bed controller and raised him to a nearly sitting position. "Here," she said as she placed a different clicker in his hand. "Use this to control the pain medicine." He clicked away and relief came quickly. He could relax a little now.

"Gillmore is under arrest and down the hall, thanks to you. His knee is trashed. Good work, mi amor."

Michael smiled as much as his battered face could manage and whispered a prayer of gratitude. "The Russians?" he asked.

"In jail."

"How?"

"There was an Interpol Incident Response Team already in Northern Ireland. They flew down and captured the baddies in time."

"How?"

Ciara just smiled. "Callahan family connections."

"Fabian called my dad."

"Yes."

"But how?" Talking was harder than he expected.

"How did they know where to go?" she asked. "I loaded a tracker app on your phone last week. And mine. And gave their codes to Fabian three days ago. Those Russian eejits didn't think to turn off our phones. The IRT was a block away when I crashed out of the warehouse."

"So, you brought in the cavalry, just like in the movies."

She nodded, smiling.

"You saved my life."

"You saved my life first, boyo."

They went silent for a few moments. Eventually, Michael snapped back to the present. "What about the girls?"

"Oh yes, the girls! That's the best part! Twelve girls were rescued, Michael. Twelve girls!" She pulled her phone from a back pocket, slid carefully onto the edge of his bed, held out the screen and pushed the play button. "Interpol is all over this now. Here's the official video showing Finnish Customs and police intercepting the first shipment in Helsinki." The picture was nighttime dark, but Michael could make out multiple armed figures wearing flak jackets escorting females to waiting vans. "And the Russian police rescued eight more in St. Petersburg and arrested the kidnappers." She laughed. "Michael, me darlin' boy, you were right. Even the Russian president is cooperating in cleaning up this mess."

Michael fell back into his pillows. A rush of emotions—relief, anger, pride, love—flowed through his fuzzy mind and battered body from head to toe. "You did it. Ciara Harrington, the Irish Wonder Woman."

"No, Michael." She shook her head, then took his hand again and kissed it. One of her fabulous smiles was there just for him. "*You* did it. You succeeded when the Interpol police and the Garda failed. You didn't give up. You, Michael Anthony Callahan. You decided something needed to be done. And when it got dangerous, you kept going. In fact, when everybody else ran away from danger, you ran to it."

"So did you."

"I wouldn't have if not for you."

"Oh yeah, you would have. Especially once you heard about the girls."

"Maybe. Anyway, we make a good team, mi amor." She shifted her position to edge a bit closer and whispered in his ear. "I met your da. I was right about him. He's a good man. And he loves you."

"My dad? Where?" Startled, Michael tried to sit up and was rewarded with another avalanche of pain. He clicked several more times.

"Shh, I told you, lie back and listen, me darlin' boy." She held a cup of water to his lips, then sat back. "Me mum and I got to meet the taoiseach, our prime minister, along with your da and your ambassador and Nathan Chismar and his da yesterday."

"Nate, too! How cool is that? How'd it go?"

"It was grand! She was ever so nice, even served us tea! Can you imagine? Me with the prime minister!" Ciara laughed at the memory. "The Minister for Justice and Equality was there—the Garda works for him—along with the Interpol police. They had been trying to bust this group for over a year.

"When you didn't call Nathan, he tried to call you. When you wouldn't answer, he called me. When I didn't answer, he went to his father who took him to the Garda and basically pounded the top sergeant's desk. One of the chaps in the office was a member of a special group, sort of a SWAT bloke. He made a few calls, and the alert went out. The Garda used Nathan's tunnel maps and arrived at the warehouse just minutes after the IRT."

"But would have been too late for us."

"Maybe. The point is that they came. The Garda is somewhat rehabilitated as a result. The minister is pleased."

They sat and pondered again what could have been, almost was. Michael said what they were thinking. "So by going to the authorities and forcing them to listen, Nate did what we couldn't do."

"Yep. Ironic, isn't it? And the best part is that the taoiseach told the minister that it was obvious that Nathan was raised by a good citizen and that the Garda should leave Mr. Chismar alone in the future."

"That's great news. Almost as great as waking up alive today."

She laughed. "I love your da. He's so much like you—kind and good-hearted." She clapped her hands. "And guess who is number one on the list of officials whose heads will roll? The méara! The taoiseach called her in and gave her a proper drubbing. The méara's history now. Done in politics."

"Anybody else?"

"Her husband, Superintendent Hallums! He's been suspended from the Garda and investigations are starting. They'll uncover every bad decision he's ever made, every bribe he's ever taken. And rumor has it that Séamus Hallums will be expelled from St. George's."

"Oh man. The sins of the father. I wouldn't wish that on anybody, not even Séamus." He winced as pain shot across his shoulders. Another click.

"Michael, you are such a push-over! Séamus gave you trouble from your first day. He learned to be an arsehole from his father."

"Maybe he can see where that will take him if he doesn't change."

Ciara shrugged. "He learned things from his father. You learned different things from your father."

"Yeah," he said. "Yeah, I did, didn't I?"

"Anyhow, Michael, we're both invited to meet the president at his official residence, *Áras an Uachtaráin*, when you get out of hospital. He wants to show his appreciation."

Ciara leaned forward. He felt her warm breath on his skin. A stray lock of her strawberry blonde hair fell over her left eye. She brushed it aside with a smile.

"Speaking of showing appreciation ..." She oh-so-carefully placed her soft lips on his dry chapped ones. She murmured, "Let me show you my appreciation."

CHAPTER FIFTY-FIVE

St. Anthony's Hospital
Dublin

The door opened. Ciara jumped to her feet and backed away from the bed. "Top of the morning to you, Mrs. Callahan," she said, face flushing.

"Good morning, Ciara, dear," Babushka said with a knowing smile. "Is the boy awake?"

"Yes, ma'am. Michael's awake and feeling better, all things considered."

Michael gave a weak wave. "Ciao, Babushka."

Babushka leaned over Michael, stroked his bandaged head, and gave him a kiss. She sat in a leather chair by the bed. "I'm happy to see you awake. You look much better than yesterday."

"I feel better than yesterday, Babushka," he said with a smile. "Way better."

"I'm getting you out of here and taking you home when the doctors permit."

Michael knew this was coming. "No, Babushka. I'm staying here to finish the school term."

She blinked and stiffened in her seat. "I don't think you heard me, young man. You *will* come home to Taos so you can get better."

"Babushka, I can get better here." He reached for Ciara's hand. "I'm staying."

The door swung open again, and Michael's father strode in. Babushka turned to him. "Tommy, Mikey says he wants to stay here."

"Michael," Ciara said.

Colonel Callahan looked puzzled.

Babushka said with a glance and a smile at Ciara, "I think our Mikey prefers to be called Michael now."

Colonel Callahan turned toward his son, leaned over, and kissed the top of his head. "Michael it is then. Michael Anthony Callahan himself. That sounds like a real Irish-American, young man."

"No, Dad." He needed to say something to his father right away. "In fact, I am a naturalized American citizen, born in Bolivia and raised in a blend of American, Irish, Italian, Australian, Russian, and Native American cultures. I am unique. I am me."

His father laughed. "That you are, my number one son. That you are. Unique is exactly the right word."

More words rushed out of Michael. "I'm sorry, Dad, for going after those guys. It was probably stupid." He paused. "Yeah, okay, it was stupid."

Colonel Callahan put his hand on Michael's shoulder. "No, son. It was the right thing to do. It was what you had to do. In fact, it was heroic."

Heroic? Did his father, a certified official, real-life action hero, actually call him heroic? Not possible. He glanced at Ciara. She was beaming.

"As for your schooling, Michael, the headmaster made a point of telling me you would be welcome to stay until end of term, as planned. I agreed."

Ciara gave a little gasp and promptly turned pink. She smiled at Michael and stroked his hand.

"So, what do you two young people have in mind for Fabian?" Colonel Callahan said, smiling.

Michael looked at Ciara. She shrugged like she had no idea what he was talking about either.

His father chuckled. "I just got off the horn with your Uncle Brian in Washington. He's walking Fabian through the State Department now, and will escort him, new passport in hand, out to Dulles Airport to catch tonight's flight to Dublin. He'll be here in time for breakfast." His father laughed at the look on Michael's face. "It seems the taoiseach wants to meet you and him, along with Nate and Ciara. All of you heroes at once."

"Awesome!" Michael said. "Ciara, it looks like you'll get to meet a certified New Mexican cowboy!" He laughed. "Fabian's never been east of the New Mexico state line. I hope he remembered to buy a new hat."

His father chuckled. "I have another idea that you two might like."

Michael waited.

"After the school term ends, why don't you invite Ciara and her family over to Taos to spend Christmas with your American-Irish-Italian-Australian-Russian and Native American family?"

Michael cheered. "Yes! I can teach her how to snowboard!"

AUTHOR'S NOTES

When I began writing *The Irish Skateboard Club*, my goal was to explore Michael Callahan's search for an identity that he could call his own—his coming-of-age journey, along with a hint of romance. Michael is a pretty talented young man, but he didn't see himself that way. Being adopted added even more questions for him. He was confused and felt he was the only one of his friends and family who didn't have it together.

He needed to prove himself to himself. So I sent him to a different country. My three previous books depicted the Callahan family as proud Irish-Americans. (Nearly one in ten Americans claims some link to Ireland). By going to Ireland, Michael would encounter another set of obstacles that would shape and define his self-image. My sons went abroad while in high school. They all say those international trips were not only killer, they helped them gain self confidence and accelerated their maturity into young adulthood.

Michael and Ciara stumbled into human trafficking by accident. Part of the reason for this book was to promote awareness of this spreading social cancer. When I first heard of human trafficking being categorized as modern day slavery, I said "What? In the twenty-first century? Not possible." Then I investigated. I was wrong. It is huge, horrific, and needs to be addressed and discussed in order to stop it. Young people—the primary targets of traffickers—need to be more aware. As do adults who deal with children and teenagers—parents, grandparents, coaches, teachers, and counselors, etc. There are more people enslaved today than ever before in the history of humankind. While organized crime is responsible for many kidnappings and much of the trafficking, a huge percentage of victims is trafficked by people they know, like boyfriends or family members. Which is hard to believe but true nonetheless.

Don't do what Michael and Ciara did in the book. Rebuffed by the fictional authorities, they tried to track down the traffickers themselves. Instead, go straight to the real-life (and serious) authorities.

There are hundreds of organizations out there working to stop trafficking. The most obvious in the USA are local and state police, the FBI, and the Department of Homeland Security. If you are overseas, you can contact your national authorities, INTERPOL, or other national police organizations like the Garda Síochána in Ireland. Do not put yourself in danger.

A simple computer search will show on-line resources like Operation Underground Railroad (O.U.R.), Airline Ambassadors International, Saved in America (SIAM), U.S. Human Trafficking Information Exchange, Thorn—founded by Demi Moore and Aston Kutcher, to name just a few. There are also organizations that have education programs and will come to your school, church, or group to pass along basic facts, tips, and strategies.

I brought in parkour because I was stunned by how powerful and athletic it was, and it seemed like something young adult readers would relate to. I was entranced by the sport and got caught up in the research—learning new things is exhilarating. I love to read books that force me to look stuff up and I try to fill my writings with "little known but interesting facts." Getting lost doing research is also why it takes me so long to write a book.

Skateboarders/snowboarders sometimes get a bum rap and often get called names like "knuckle draggers," "troublemakers," etc. I had the pleasure to work with snowboarders from all over New Mexico and at the national level with the United States of America Snowboard and Free Ski Association (USASA) for more than a decade. I met many skateboarders along the way as well since the two sports are populated by like-minded athletes, many of whom both skate and shred. Most of the kids were great, some not so much. It's similar with pro athletes. They sometimes show up in the news acting like thugs or hoodlums—and yet there are many others who have foundations to promote worthy causes, work with disadvantaged children, promote equality, etc. That seems to be the way of the world—most people are pretty nice, some aren't.

The first time I flew an airplane to Europe, my track took me over Ireland. The island filled my entire windscreen and I was mesmerized by how gorgeous it was, with so many different hues of green. It was stunning. Michael's reaction in the book mirrors my own. Despite what I wrote about Ireland looking flat to Michael, there are lumpy parts of beautiful, wild terrain that are not very high, but pass for mountains in Ireland. And yes, it rains a lot.

While *The Irish Skateboard Club* is a work of fiction, I tried to be as accurate about details as possible. Sometimes, though, details get in the way and authors have to invoke the convenient expedient of "poetic license" and basically make stuff up to make the story work. For example, there are lots of tunnels under and around Dublin, and, as I state in the text, even some cool YouTube videos of these tunnels. There are no tunnels that I know of as convenient to the Port of Dublin as I portray.

I visited Ireland a couple times way back in the 20th century and found the Irish people to be delightful, welcoming, and fun. Dublin is an amazing place. I can't wait to visit again, this time for longer!

ABOUT THE AUTHOR

Brinn Colenda is a former military pilot and the author of The Callahan Family Saga, an awarding-winning political-military series.

He and his wife, Lindy, divide their time between the United States, the Republic of Panama, and international locations yet to be discovered.

You can follow Brinn on Facebook at Brinn Colenda Author. His website is www.brinncolenda.us

SUGGESTED DISCUSSION POINTS

Michael states that he's going to Ireland to absorb Irish culture in order to fit in the Callahan family. Is his motivation valid? In the end, has he accomplished what he set out to do?

How is Michael a typical teenager? What makes him unique?

Why is Michael unhappy about whom he perceives himself to be? How does his perception reflect reality and differ from it?

In what ways has Michael resolved his identity crisis? How will Michael's life be different as a result of his adventures in Ireland?

How would you characterize Michael's relationships with the adults in his life. Do the same for Ciara.

Retell the main points of the book from the viewpoint of Michael's father or mother.

Is Michael's goal of coaching in the X-Games and/or the Olympics realistic? What are the advantages of setting high goals?

What effect does skateboarding have on Michael's life?

How has Michael affected the lives of Ciara and Nathan?

Did Michael make the right decision to take on the Russian Mafiya? What might have been a safer way to handle it? What would you have done?

Should Michael have told his parents about the Russian smugglers? Why or why not?

Examine Fabian's role in the book.

Were Michael and Ciara correct in involving Nathan in a dangerous venture?

In the real world, how would you recognize a person who is being trafficked? Where could you go to find information of what to do if you suspect human trafficking? What sources of info are there regarding trafficking? Which law enforcement agencies? Web sites? On-line organizations? International organizations?

If you had the opportunity to study abroad, would you take it? Why or why not? If so, where would you like to go and why?

Callahan Family Saga
by Brinn Colenda

Political-Military Thrillers are available from

Southern Yellow Pine Publishing

www.syppublishing.com

or Amazon and Barnes&Noble

The year is 1999. Kurt Wallerein, feared, hated and hunted by every intelligence service and law enforcement agency in the West forms a partnership with an embattled Fidel Castro. Their goal is to destabilize the democratic governments in South America—and the United States.

Lieutenant Colonel Tom Callahan, USAF and his compadres in the U.S. Military Group-Bolivia risk their lives and reputations battling enemies—foreign and domestic—in this exciting novel.

Colenda's thriller is a sensation. He owes me for a month's worth of adrenaline that I used up reading his book—all without getting off the couch. And the scary part? The plot is all too plausible.

—Scott Archer Jones, award-winning author of
A Rising Tide of People Swept Away

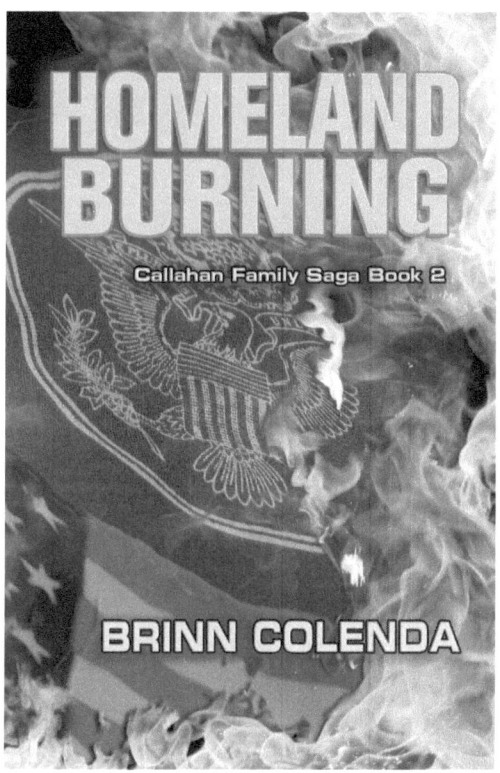

Spring of 2000: Wildfires destroy mountain watersheds and municipal water systems, breached dams release tidal waves of water to obliterate farms and towns, and stone-cold shooters target helpless civilians as environmental terrorism comes to the United States.

Kurt Wallerein, the world's foremost terrorist-for-hire, unleashes a terrifying campaign of attacks on the American homeland...and his greatest enemy, Air Force Colonel Tom Callahan.

Callahan must rally support to stop the attacks, but his political enemies in Washington conspire to distract the President and ridicule evidence, forcing Callahan to go rogue. What will it take to stop Wallerein?

In *Homeland Burning*, Brinn Colenda delivers an epic story about the conflict between good and evil. You will love his characters and find yourself on a dizzying roller coaster ride of action and suspense. Be prepared to lose sleep over this one. Highly recommended.

—Joseph Badal, Tony Hillerman Award Winner and Amazon #1 Best-Selling Author of *Sins of the Fathers*.

Were American POWs left behind at the end of the Vietnam War—either by accident or by design?

Colonel Tom Callahan is driven to find out—his own father is still listed as Missing In Action. What Callahan doesn't understand is how politically explosive the issue is, domestically and internationally. As he begins his quest, friends and associates meet violent deaths. His journey takes him halfway across the world to Vietnam, China, Mongolia, and ultimately, Siberia. He is helped and hindered by unexpected friends and cunning, deadly enemies.

"Brinn Colenda once again proves himself to be a master storyteller…action and adventure with an intricate storyline…expertly researched…a tale of intrigue and conspiracy that will keep you reading late into the night!"

—Walter E. Buchanan III, Lieutenant General, USAF (ret)

*Author's Note: Michael Callahan is introduced in *Chita Quest* as an active—and important—four-year-old boy

www.ingramcontent.com/pod-product-compliance
Lightning Source LLC
LaVergne TN
LVHW041624060526
838200LV00040B/1424